Álvaro
Cunqueiro

Folks From Here and There

ÁLVARO CUNQUEIRO

Folks From Here and There

Translated from Galician by Kathleen March

XUNTA DE GALICIA

Small Stations Press

Small Stations Press
Registered address: 20 Dimitar Manov Street, 1408 Sofia, Bulgaria
You can order books and contact the publisher at
www.smallstations.com

First published as *Xente de aquí e de acolá* by Editorial Galaxia in 1971

This English edition first published in 2011, reprinted in 2017
ISBN 978-954-384-009-0 (paperback original)
ISBN 978-954-384-070-0 (reprint edition)

Contents

Author's Note

My friends Antonio Odriozola and Francisco Fernández del Riego gathered many of the "portraits" that make up this book, which were strewn about in various magazines and journals. Without their help, the harvest, and also the gleaning, would not have been possible. That's why I want both of their names to appear here. I am grateful to them and this collection of "inventions" is dedicated to them.

Letter the Author Sent to Dr Domingo García-Sabell While
He Was Putting Together This Book

My Dear Domingo,

*You once wrote about me that I used to come up to you
and stand there staring at you or other people and it seemed
like I'd traveled a long way, was a bit disoriented and slow
in recognizing you and figuring out where I was. Since
you're the one who said it, there must have been a lot of
truth to it. Well, I could tell you I'd just been with these folks,
the ones I'm talking about in the pages that follow. Now did
they exist or do they? Somebody might say, without giving
it much thought, that they never existed before, nor do they
now, since I made them up. And that someone would call the
case closed, but I don't think you would, nor would I. That's
why I'm writing to you, so you'll help me not just to figure
out whether these folks existed or not, but also to decide if
they resemble my stories in any way. I want to know if there's
much of a difference between the real one and the imaginary
one, or more: if the folks I've created are Galician or not,
and what they tell us about Galicians, if indeed they're from
that part of the world.*

*Because I'm convinced these are portraits of people who
are members of our tribe, and they couldn't be from just any
tribe. Which means, in my opinion, that they all have an ounce
of every facet of Galician identity and the whole Galician*

structure is spread out among them, their ways of sizing up the world, their lively imaginations, the meanderings of their dreams and desires, their sharp wit, their penchant for surprise, the irony that, at any given moment, can turn a man into a king, and the humble nature, the rich flavor of laziness, the complaining about diseases they don't have and dying at the hands of their obsession, bequeathing it to the next one, like a secret treasure... I could go on, saying what I think they're made of, but I don't dare unless you help me a little with your scientific knowledge. There are some who try, justifiably so, to understand what the Galician is like from the angle of other realities, ones more within their reach, because those realities are part of their daily experiences. But I go and try to dig into the Galician identity until I find those secret spaces. When I see certain Galicians hoeing those personal rows, I'm right in thinking that they're digging the way only Galicians do. The Galician has a distinct sort of imagination. Do Galicians dream, hope, feel surprise, believe, differently than the Catalonians perhaps? And am I, the researcher, an authentic Galician when I tell their stories, half believing, half joking? If this were so, dear Domingo, if these traits were a way of being Galician and I told it in the Galician style, wouldn't whoever read this book of mine know more about Galicians after reading it?

I cannot "think deep" – that great Saturday-barber's term invented by Castelao – about the task because I'm neither anthropologist nor sociologist, I'm not even an expert in comparative folklore and certainly no scientist. I'm just a person who spends time with our folks and tells stories.

With some of them, since I'm asking you if they existed or not and then, not being very sure, I end up asking myself – and asking you – if there ever even was, or wasn't, an Álvaro Cunqueiro. How could I know that much about these folks if they never existed, if they don't exist now, unless I hadn't been or don't exist now. It's a really hard nut to crack and I'm not asking you just one question, but two or three. When you have a free moment, do answer me, since you must have figured out I'm a bit worried about this matter and I need to know from the horse's mouth, from an expert, if these folks are anything like their portraits and if I'm one of them or not because I fancy myself the narrator of so many lives and miracles – and if I can reveal all of this, which is almost like it's from the netherworld, does it mean I have a habit of spending time outside this world, investigating? Investigating the secret of what a Galician is?

Best regards from your eternal friend,
Álvaro Cunqueiro

Mondoñedo, June 1971

Somoza of Leiva

Yesterday I went into a bar that had twelve pictures on the walls, printed in Berlin in 1899, which told the story of Hernán Cortés with the conquest of Mexico and that gentleman's love affair with the "interpreter" Marina. And that reminded me of Somoza of Leiva. This fellow Somoza, who was from Leiva – Leiva is on a high hill, surrounded by chestnut trees, in Terra de Miranda, and I never saw a place with so many fountains – had served the king in the Otumba Regiment and since then he'd had a soft spot in his heart for the Marquis of the Valley of Oaxaca and his Mexican adventures and knew all there was to know about the Sad Night. In Lugo he'd purchased those same twelve pictures I was staring at now in the tavern and he had them by the stairs and dining room of the place. When I was a boy, I went there to the feast of St Bartholomew and Somoza, who was already limping some from the time an otter bit him in the ford by Sigüeiro, would read the text of each episode to me and he was surprised that I would read the French to him, since the writing at the bottom of each picture was in two languages.

"Look at those fat legs!"

And he'd point out Marina's round, white legs to me. Marina was looking at herself in a mirror the Spanish captain had given her.

Somoza was a memoranda writer, an untrained expert and a shyster. He made a trip to Baños de Molgas and brought back an odd dog that had yellow fur with black spots, a white backside, and lifted its hind legs to pee. It was a sad, silent dog that ate the apples that fell from the trees in the meadow and when it heard bees buzzing, it'd try to trap them, lying in wait, as if they were partridges.

"That dog's worthless!" my cousin from Trasmontes told Somoza.

"Well, it's the best sort of dog a lawyer can have!" Somoza replied.

And he went and explained to my cousin that it was the smartest dog he'd ever known and that for a lawyer from Lugo like Pepe Bonito or from Madrid like Soto Reguera it was priceless.

"It's a dog that only barks at the other side in a legal suit!"

If Somoza was working on a villager's case and someone came over for a consultation and the dog started barking, it meant that the visitor was not trustworthy and had come to meddle in the affair. The dog identified the favorable witnesses and the ones for the opposing side or the false ones. It was never wrong. When the dog got sick and went blind, Somoza took it to Lugo, to Gasalla the eye doctor. He carried it in a basket, wrapped in a blanket from Zamora. They were crossing Santo Domingo Square when the dog barked from inside the basket. Somoza stopped and looked to see what was happening and the municipal guard from Crecente, who'd fined him, was going by, heading toward San Marcos Street.

I forgot to mention that the dog's name was Montezuma.

Pontes of Meirado

I met Pontes of Meirado many years ago. He was a grown man already. Since he was seventeen, he'd smoked a pipe and worn a hat. Tall, thin, dark, always sniffling, he wrapped his long neck in a scarf with green and red stripes and had a large Adam's apple, angular and hairy, which was always moving. When he smoked, he blew smoke constantly out of his mouth and nostrils and, I think, from his ears and eyes. His hat was always perched on his head, swallowed up in the thick smoke. And his raspy voice emerged like from a deep cave when he gave his view on the antipodes, which he didn't believe in. Pontes' big argument was about sliding: if an aurora borealis falls down and slides while searching for an aurora australis, there'll be a point when the soles of their feet touch. These two would be his antipodes. Now then, has anybody heard of someone slipping upward? The ones who talk about antipodes talk as if the earth were perfectly flat, and the world is round. In the barbershops, that was a much discussed topic.

Pontes insisted that he'd go to the lectures given in Buenos Aires by a German on the magnetic center of the earth, which is in the shape of a pear, and if the part about the magnet were true, then there really could be antipodes. The magnet, according to the German, took a while to form and until it was fully solidified, the earth, flying around the sun, went around dripping parts off its lower side, parts that can now be found on other planets: for example, a cherry tree on the moon or some sheep on Mars.

Pontes, whose first name was Manuel, returned from Argentina to see about an inheritance and while he was in

bed with a bad cold, he remembered a girlfriend he'd had in
Mar del Plata, an Italian lass called Virna Filossi, and sent
papers to his brother Adolfo so he could marry her by proxy.
But Adolfo liked the girl, threw the papers into the garbage
and married the Calabrian girl himself. Pontes never got over
that blow, even though Adolfo disappeared and he never had
to give his brother his part of the inheritance. He told me
about his love life in a tavern in Campo Castillo, in Lugo,
while eating partridge. He'd grasp the partridge carefully by
the neck and legs and sigh:

"There never was a more lovely traitress!"

After a moment's pause, he'd sink his long, flat teeth into
the bird's breast.

Nothing more was ever heard about Adolfo or Virna.
I told him, as a joke, that maybe, since the earth's central
magnet wasn't in place, they'd fallen off the planet and were
roaming around the moon.

"I'm the only one who'd know how to make that trip."

And from the inside pocket of his leather jacket he'd take
out a handkerchief embroidered with little blue flowers, a
gift Virna had given him. He'd rub it over his nose and eyes.
Over his nose, so he could recall the scent of his lost lover;
over his eyes, so he could dry his big, bitter tears.

Penedo of Alduxe

When I read in Lady Augusta Gregory that there was a Golden Mantle associated by Gaels with the myth of the Speckled Jewel, I'd already heard of its existence thanks to my friend Penedo of Alduxe, Pedro Anido García. I owe him and the ferryman Felipe of Amancia, who sailed the narrow part of the Miño River, a lot. They taught me how to tell stories and if I didn't learn the art better, it was my fault, not theirs. Penedo knew all the stories about Meira, from the dwarves of the abbots and Santa María Real to the mysterious blacksmiths at Pé da Serra, including the lost treasures of the marshlands. Penedo knew that the famous Golden Mantle had been kept in Meira for several centuries and that, although it'd mysteriously disappeared, that didn't mean it had left the region. It must be hanging in some secret closet, or maybe it's buried, or maybe it's submerged in water. Although I'm not saying there's no such thing as a flying closet... Penedo had actually seen the Golden Mantle. One day like any other he lay down and dreamed that a dwarf belonging to the Meira abbot was scratching his back. He dreamed so much about the Cistercians' chamber dwarves that they were always obedient and punctual for his sessions of nocturnal fantasy. The dwarf scratched with both hands, with two thumbs, since this seems to be the proper way to scratch, not scraping. Penedo dreamed that the dwarf was scratching him and at the best part he went and stopped and knelt down.

"And then," Penedo told me, "I woke up. The dwarf was at the foot of my bed. He was like a little dog, except he had a soul, was wearing green breeches and had dark eyes.

And I went and told him to scratch me because I wanted to continue sleeping, but he told me he couldn't scratch because I wasn't asleep. When I told the priest at Vilares about this, he said I hadn't understood him, unless it had been a metaphysical dwarf. Well, anyway, the dwarf didn't scratch me and I couldn't go back to sleep. And that was when the Golden Mantle appeared at the window. It was as round as a full moon, golden, shining, floating about in the breeze. It smelled like incense. The dwarf signaled to me to kneel down like he'd done. The mantle entered the room and moved forward up along the ceiling, then suddenly it rested on my shoulders. Because it hadn't slid on quite right, I went and stuck my hands out to adjust it better and the mantle flew off…"

"And didn't it even leave a trace?"

Penedo stuck his hand in his vest pocket and took out a little package of Rey de Espadas tobacco. He didn't have any paper. He showed me the yellow threads inside.

"When it left, it got caught in the branch of a fig tree for a moment and these threads were left behind. A silversmith from Lugo told me they're made of gold, of the same quality as Carolean coins."

In Ireland some people believe the mantle belonged to St Patrick, who left it for when he came back to his beloved island on Judgment Day. On the other hand, some are sure it was the mantle of King Nuga, who wore it when it had been raining for several weeks. Then the clouds, thinking the sun was irritated, fled to the sea and the sun would shine on Erin and all its green hills… I looked at Penedo with respect, for he was the only mortal of our time who'd had the Golden Mantle of the saints and mysterious abbots of old on his shoulders. We were probably in Pacios, on the bridge, watching the river flow by with its green, green waters and the seaweed growing contentedly along the bottom.

Liñas of Eirís

I have told about the forest of Eirís more than once, about those steep paths going up to the top, to the fields in Miranda, the open fields known as the King's Meadow. Here and there, heather, thorny *xesta* bushes, small oaks, thick gorse and birch trees leaning to the north because of the strong wind, which around there is called the Meira Wind and is the father of many rainstorms. On the way down to Sareiro, you see Eirís' twelve houses at the foot of the *castro*, the pre-Roman village. The house next to the bridge belongs to the Liñas family. Some still call it the Tavern and perhaps it was on the King's Highway to Lugo way back when. I was friends with Mr Ramón of the Liñas family. All the Liñases are tall, strong, blond, with blue eyes. There's a lot of Swabian blood in those parts. Mr Ramón was a hunter and amateur veterinarian who liked to prescribe mustard plasters and Tres Cepas cognac to patients. He believed in the virtues of May rains and the new moon. He also advised the sick person to dream that he was healthy.

"Dream that you've recovered and you're running a race with me!"

And to encourage the patient he'd start running down the road, spinning around in the air from time to time like a professional dancer. Sometimes, with that treatment alone, the patient would recover. He charged them coffee because according to him it was cleaner than charging money.

One day Mr Ramón was on his way to the fair at Augaxosa and in the middle of the road he found a new hat, a pearl-gray hat. He couldn't leave it there in the mud, so he took off his beret, placed it in the pocket of his sheepskin jacket and put the hat on.

"Finders keepers," he told me.

The first day he wore it, Mr Ramón realized he had a whimsical hat on, especially when greeting people. Mr Ramón liked to doff his hat when the priest of Muxueira came along on his mare and he couldn't pull it off his head. On the other hand, Freixín of Marco would go by, with whom he'd had a legal battle about the rights to use a path to drive a cart through, which he'd lost, but the hat lifted itself up. Freixín looked at Liñas and said mockingly:

"Well, I never knew you were that humble!"

Mr Ramón turned red and lowered his head. Damn hat! Nor could he greet the girls from Rancaño who were buying some *rosca* cakes from Ribadeo. But the hat greeted the beggars.

"That didn't matter to me," was Liñas' comment, "since a poor person after all is like a saint."

At home, Liñas hung the hat on the wall clock and when he hung it there, this question slipped out:

"So who was your owner?"

Mr Ramón gave two thumps to his heart. It was a typical gesture of his.

"Did it answer you?"

"It said, 'I belong to the secretary.'"

A few days later, Mr Ramón realized that the hat would go out for a stroll at the end of the day. It would go through the threshing area, slowly, and afterward perch on the branch of an apple or a fig tree. When he saw all this, Mr Ramón didn't dare wear it, but when he was sleeping, the hat jumped off its perch and went to rest on Liñas' face. The hat, thought Mr Ramón, was full of hot air and nearly suffocated the medicine man.

"I'm fed up with this!" Mr Ramón said to it one night.

"Well, I'm leaving this place then!" answered the hat.

And it left. Mr Ramón ran after it as far as the doorway of his house. The hat was traveling about three yards above the floor, in a tilted position.

"Like a tall fellow was wearing the hat at a rakish angle!"

When it reached the crossroads, it didn't seem to know which way to go, but finally it headed along the road to Meira.

"I'm telling you, it was going along like a real dandy."

Mr Ramón told me this story in confidence and because I promised never to put it down on paper. That must have been thirty years ago. We were sitting in the place where they do the washing, next to the embankment at the mill. From time to time, an apple would fall into the water.

Penedo of Rúa

I had to make a recommendation for a grandson of Penedo of Rúa. Penedo had once spoken with a crow.

"Don't trust your lawyer!" said the crow to Penedo from the crook of a tree while he was planting.

And in fact Penedo did not trust his lawyer, who seemed to be having conversations with the other party in the case. Penedo scratched his head.

"And the judge?" he asked the crow.

The crow beat its wings, but didn't move from the branch. It responded in a sour voice:

"There are hams that fix legal cases!"

The next day Penedo hitched up his mare and went to Lugo. He left the animal at the Casa Quintela inn and, without stopping to wet his whistle, went to see Pepe Benito. The great leader of the people of Lugo looked at him with his bright, laughing eyes and smiled:

"That crow from Rúa is a really smart crow!"

"Yes, sir, it knew I was involved in a legal matter."

Pepe Benito took on Penedo's case, managed it very knowledgeably and won.

"Now," he said to Penedo when he went to pay him, "you should go find that crow and offer it at least half a bushel of wheat."

Penedo walked around all the threshing area, shouting to the crow that he'd won the suit, to see if he could find his black-feathered advisor. In the village they thought that Penedo had gone mad with the excitement of winning the case in court. But Penedo was a grateful man and wanted to pay the crow its half a bushel of wheat, just as Don José

Benito Pardo had suggested. Finally, one day in a fallow field, on one of those hills beside the Lea, with grain growing up on top for turtledoves and the meadow residents below, paradise for hoopoes – "hup! hup!" – happy with the arrival of spring and feasting on the first crickets as soon as they come out to sing on warm days, a crow answered him.

"I won the suit!" shouted Penedo.

"Congratulations!" responded the crow.

Penedo said that, if it was going to be there the next day, he'd bring it half a bushel of wheat. The crow told him it'd really appreciate it. When he went the next day, the crow told Penedo it'd like some coffee cake if he had any left from the feast of St Martin.

"And you could buy me a hat for the winter!"

Penedo was very grateful. He went down to Mondoñedo to see Mr Domingo, the hatter whose shop was in the arcade on the main square. Mr Domingo made a cap for the crow, using the measurements of a pigeon. A lined cap with a sequined ribbon.

"It'll look quite fancy!" said the hatter.

"It's a very human crow!"

Penedo took the cap to the crow and the bird, to thank him, once it had it on and it looked really nice, said:

"You have to go look for a treasure over in Braña!"

So Penedo went to Braña and between two oak trees found something made of metal, but nobody in the village knew what machine it came from, nor what it was for. This was over eighty years ago. Penedo took the thing to the fair at Vilalba to show it to a friend of his who was a watchmaker.

"That's a bicycle pedal, you know!"

There wasn't even a bicycle in the region. The pedal was completely new. The watchmaker had to explain to Penedo what a bicycle was.

"So is it a treasure or not?" Penedo asked the watchmaker.

"Well, a treasure, it's not exactly a treasure, but it sure is a mystery!"

Penedo wrapped it up in a handkerchief and went to Braña to bury it where he'd found it. He died a short while after, not knowing for sure what a bicycle was like and how it could have a man atop it and travel along. They buried Penedo, like all the Penedos, in the little cemetery in Rúa, with the big yew tree by the gate that almost covers the whole thing.

Louzao of Mouride

This fellow Manuel Costa, alias Louzao of Mouride, considered himself to be a relative of mine because both of us were born at eight in the morning on the 22nd of December, under the sign of Capricorn. And he believed in horoscopes.

"I like to think we'll both be very successful in diplomacy matters!" he'd say to me and slap his throat two or three times.

When he was fifteen, he emigrated to Buenos Aires and started work as a kitchen assistant in a bakery. In a short time he'd mastered the art of the Neapolitan pizza and knew the right amount of oregano to use, which is the most difficult part, besides how to make good dough. And he married a daughter of the owner named Vittoria.

"When you write my story," Louzao told me, "make sure you put two *t*s in Vittoria."

I've done just that: Vittoria. They were very happy during the first few months of their marriage. Vittoria did Louzao's hair with a styling gel that smelled like strawberries and sang Neapolitan songs to him. One day at the bread shop Louzao didn't feel well and asked permission to go home. When he got there, he couldn't find Vittoria. He lay down in bed and an hour later his wife arrived. She was dressed like a firefighter. Vittoria confessed: she was on the list as a firefighter in Los Toldos and had to work Tuesdays, Thursdays and Saturdays. They thought she was a man there and she was called Gasparo Ponti. She earned a salary and had an ID card with covers made of red oilcloth. Vittoria confessed to her husband that she liked nothing more in the world than to watch a fire burn and, after watching the flames, to dress like a man. In a trunk in the back room she kept half a dozen men's outfits. Louzao tried to prevent her from engaging in that diversion, but she refused.

"She wanted to hit me over the head with a chair!"

Louzao told the story to everyone in the bakery and his wife got mad and walked out. Louzao was left in the kitchen, crying with little Michelangelo, who was eight months old, on his lap. Vittoria took the trunk with the men's suits and Louzao never heard from her again. She wasn't with the firefighters of Los Toldos, nor on any of the lists in the capital city. But she must be in some fire-fighting company in the Republic.

Saddened, Louzao decided to return to Mouride and bought half of his brother Pedro's mill in Seixos. He religiously paid the monthly subscription to two newspapers in Buenos Aires.

"In case there's a fire, you know!"

And that was what he read about in the papers, just the fires, to see if somewhere Vittoria, with a double *t*, had been mentioned. In his mind, his wife became an almost mythical goddess fire-douser. If there happened to be a fire in Coruña or Madrid, Louzao would say:

"If my Vittoria were there, she'd put it out in a jiffy!"

Years went by. Michelangelo had turned eighteen. He was another Capricorn, like his father and me, and so, according to astrology, was destined to have great triumphs in diplomacy. He was a simpleton with huge dark eyes. When he came with his father to Mondoñedo, I'd give him a stick of licorice, taken from the pharmacy, and Miguel Angel would drool yellow for half an hour... One day Louzao heard from Buenos Aires. His brother-in-law Francesco Luigi had written to him and informed him that he was sending a trunk; at the same time he told him that Vittoria had died of tuberculosis.

The trunk was delivered by the Sons of Estanislao Durán of Vigo. They brought it in a car from the junction in Moncelos to Mouride. All the Louzaos were present when Mr Manuel opened it. Women's clothing, some packages of yerba mate, a revolver, four or five pairs of men's pants and the uniform of the firefighters of Los Toldos, plus the helmet, axe and belt with treble hook. Miguel Angel started to cry when he saw the helmet and didn't stop until they let him put it on. They couldn't get it off him. He went to work in the fields with it on, went to bring in the cows and take the milk to the fair at Meira. When he was supposed to do his military service, they thought he was crazy. He died a few months later. His father, who understood, let him be put in the casket wearing the helmet. On a gold-colored plaque made of tin you could see the words: "Firefighters of Los Toldos. First Brigade."

Mel of Vincios

When I wrote my *Medicine Men's School*, I forgot Mel of Vincios, Pita of San Cobade and a disciple of Mel, a fellow named Lousas. (I don't know whether he's dead or alive, he's the one who told me about his teacher, who I never met.) Mel of Vincios, who came from Oscos – which is where the Marquis of Sargadelos was from – was a tall, thin fellow with a beard that reached all the way to his waist. When a photographer set up a studio in Ribadeo at the end of the last century, Mel of Vincios took his patients who had a bit of extra money so they could get their picture taken and several of them got much better. He'd chase small demons out of people's bodies by saying their names out loud, their first and last names, plus their nicknames. The demon inside the patient would kick and spit.

"Mel," Lousas told me, "kept shouting the nicknames and would kick the demon in the mouth."

"The demon?" I asked, surprised.

"Well, the patient got a kick or two as well."

The demon ended up leaving and the ailing person was relieved. It seems the cure consists of knowing the name of the demon living inside us; once it's known what the demon living inside somebody is called, the horned one has no choice but to go away.

Mel was very learned in matters of bones. The first thing he'd do when he saw a patient was to count his bones and straighten out the ones that were loose or a bit twisted. They said Mel of Vincios had the ability to be everywhere at once and that, while he was in Riotorto, straightening out one fellow's collarbone, at the same time he was in Trabada, listening to another's belly.

"Is that really true?" I asked Lousas.

"Hey, what do you mean 'true'? Who knows what scientific advances there will be in the future?"

Mel often talked in verse and for entire days. He wrote crime stories for blind people. There was a crime in Tapia de Casariego and Mel made a rhyme about it and at the end, in six quatrains, he put the descriptions of the suspects, well disguised, of course, without giving their names. The prosecutor in Oviedo read Mel's ballad, studied the clues and informed the police, who located the criminal. Mel went to Oviedo when they took the oral deposition and people applauded him in court. He spent four days in Oviedo at the invitation of the private prosecutor. During the final years of his life, Mel retired from medicine and devoted himself to legal cases. He had a lot of them and lost the majority. He became fond of hanging around lawyers' offices. He went from Oscos to Ribadeo on horseback, riding through the dark Garganta gorge. He invented claims, inheritances and indictments, just so he could have conversations with the lawyers, who found it hard to get beyond Mel of Vincios' argumentative imagination. They say he used to return to Oscos with a smile on his face.

"Because of me Cuervo the notary from Ribadeo isn't going to sleep for a month!" he said.

After he died, the people in Oscos and the blacksmiths of Taramundi on their way to the market at Veiga saw him walking through the woods, collecting herbs. Wearing the same peaked cap and fur-lined leather jacket, he was with his dog named Ney, who was also dead, hunting partridges in the high pastures of Prior.

Novo of Parmuide

A nephew of Novo of Parmuide, who was about to embark on the Portuguese packet ship *Santa María*, came to my house in Vigo. I asked him what was new while reminding him that I hadn't been to Xerás or Parmuide in over twenty years. You cross the river by a wooden bridge and the road enters Parmuide, going past some fields that have big puddles in autumn and winter, where the dry oak leaves float.

"The swing's there in the attic!" he told me.

Novo, his uncle – may he rest in peace – having first seen a swing and see-saw as a little boy at the St Luke fair in Mondoñedo or the St Froilan festivities in Lugo, got the idea to have first the swing, then the see-saw. He'd go to any festival and spend everything he had on swings. When he returned from military service, which he did in the Farnesio Cavalry in Valladolid, he brought back a single swing with chains and a seat lined with green corduroy and trimmed with bells. He went and set it up in the threshing area and whenever he had time, he'd get on it and swing. He took naps in the swing and when he wanted to establish a friendship with somebody, he'd invite him to swing as well. I don't know when Novo, who'd had a corporal in Valladolid who had re-enlisted and knew how to cure the horses of his regiment and had passed the prescriptions along to my neighbor, noticed that his swing had medicinal properties. At the beginning he only cured colds with a few doses of the swing, but afterward he offered it for headaches, liver fever, insomnia, the anemia they call "being delicate" and childhood rickets, whether caused by melancholy or being finicky. He came to have quite a lot of customers. He left the farming to his brothers, bought an alarm clock with a double alarm and devoted himself exclusively to the art of curing people. Once, around the feast of San Pedro de Riotorto, he called me aside when it was time for dessert at my uncle Serxio's house. He wanted me to collaborate with him.

"And what can I do?" I asked him.

"Pick out a few good words for me, you know!"

What he wanted, then, was for me to write some verses and find him some Latinisms – "divine words," of course – so he could recite them while pushing patients in the swing. He explained to me that the swing itself had the ability to cure people, but he wanted to spruce things up a bit because others who were not so good at healing had scientific speeches to go along with it.

"A well recited sonnet makes people more trusting!" he argued.

I let myself be talked into it and wrote some verses for him – I wish I'd kept a copy – and Novo of Parmuide memorized them. I found him some Latin phrases from Ovid. He asked for the verses in Spanish. Novo's reputation traveled far. On nights with a full moon, this medicine man had pregnant women swinging and afterward their deliveries went well. They'd come from Asturias; once they brought him a nun from Luarca who was paralyzed and she got off the swing under her own power. She was from Seville. Novo made a little money and dressed in black and instead of a beret he wore a hat. One day I was having lunch in Casa Paramés in Lugo and Novo came in.

"You know what? Now, so nobody'll learn them by heart, I recite the verses backward."

And this is what Novo of Parmuide's nephew is complaining about, because he's certain that, if his uncle had taught him the verses, he would have taken over the swing business and wouldn't have had to emigrate to Venezuela.

"If only we knew where he got those magic words from!" he told me.

I'm afraid to tell him the magic words were ones I made up and weren't secret or magic... When Novo died, the swing lost its power to cure people. It's up there in the attic, covered with dust, its bells silent, unless a mouse scurries across them. Novo's widow raises her head and makes the sign of the cross when she hears the bells tinkle.

Bouso's Head

In *The New York Times* I read that a man from Chicago, who appeared to be the son of Italians, had his head operated on and they discovered a rare extra bone in it. This had already happened in my province of Mondoñedo to Bouso of Prado. The bone from Chicago was a sort of bean-like thing situated between the parietals. Nobody knew where Bouso's bone had come from because he expelled it through his nose. But the story must be told from the beginning. *Voici des détails exacts.* Bouso was in Vilalba, at the main fair, eating octopus, and he had no choice but to argue with a table companion who was not from around there, a tall, slim, dark fellow. It later turned out he was a Valencian who'd come to buy some mules because he had gotten some from the region before that were pretty tame. Bouso and the other guy argued about the quality of the octopus and the Valencian went and said that Galicians eat shit, pardon my French, and threw his own plate down, then spat on Bouso's. Bouso got up and reached for his cane, but the Valencian was quicker. He put his hands on his neck and shook his head. Bouso felt like all his bones were coming loose inside and that, when they came loose, they made a noise like little spoons having a party inside a crystal glass. His eyes clouded over and he crumpled to the ground. He regained consciousness and was able to walk home. But his bones were loose inside his head. He could definitely hear them. He'd shake his head and the neighbors could hear them too. His wife took him to Primo of Baltar. His wife had to go with him because sometimes one of the loose bones got stuck in an eye and wouldn't let him see straight. Of course all they had to do to make the bone change its position was to give his head a good shake, but it also happened that others would stick in its place and he'd be blind until he was given another shaking.

Primo of Baltar, who was a highly respected bone-setter, told Bouso that the first thing was to shake his head backward because, since it was the wider part, the bones would be more comfortable there. And he shook it like he said he would. After that, and for two days in a row, neither one of them stopping to eat, the scientist and patient, who didn't drink either and had their shoes off, Primo put patches of hot wax on the back of his head so that, when the wax went into the skull, it would stick the bones together and also to what Primo called the "bell dome" that some people have, Bouso being one of them. The ones who dream they can hear the wind blowing are the ones that have it. When the sticking part was done, Bouso and Primo ate a roasted kid and drank half a jug of wine. Primo charged him a hundred and twenty-seven pesetas, of which twenty-seven were for the wax. Bouso also provided the goat, wine, bread, coffee and cognac. And he gave Primo a tie with a portrait of Machado that a nephew of his had sent him from Havana.

Bouso was fine after that. Every single Saturday his wife would put a patch of wax on the back of his head to fix the bones more firmly. But one came loose. It was the size of a cigarette, long and round. Bouso could definitely feel it. You could almost say he could see it. He was pruning, his mind on something else, and felt the bone move from the back of his head and hit his forehead. Crack! He had to go back to Baltar so Primo could study the situation.

"That's an extra bone you have," said the bone-setter.

"What do you mean 'extra'?" Bouso was surprised.

"It's the mercury bone, my man. It's an extra in all the people who have it."

Primo poured pipe tobacco into a sieve and made Bouso sniff it like snuff. That caused him to sneeze strongly and on the third sneeze the bone came out from up above. It looked like the bone of a chicken wing and was quite clean and white.

"It doesn't look like it's a human bone!" was Bouso's remark.

"That's why it's an extra one!" agreed Primo.

Primo said the best thing was to bury the bone so there wouldn't be an epidemic, because mercury bones are contagious. Bouso was cured. His head feels heavy and tilts backward. But that's natural because that's where all the bones are stuck together.

Xacinto the Umbrella

Guerreiro of Noste was going through the woods, crossing the range they call Arneiro, when he ran into a man who was carrying an enormous umbrella, taller than he was and made of ash-colored fabric. Guerreiro said hello to him and was surprised by the size of the umbrella, the likes of which he'd never seen before.

"That's nothing!" said the man, who was chubby and red-faced and had a big moustache.

And he showed Guerreiro the handle of the umbrella, which was a human face with a beard and eyes made of glass, and the mouth, red and open, which looked like a real live man's.

"What a mouth!" said Guerreiro.

"Umbrella, stick your tongue out!" said the man in Spanish.

And the umbrella stuck its tongue out of its mouth – it was long and red like a dog's – and licked the little man's hand very affectionately. The man took off his beret and held it in front of Guerreiro, who tossed a peseta coin into it.

"What's the trick?" asked Guerreiro, who was a very curious fellow.

The man laughed.

"There's no trick, man, it's my brother-in-law Xacinto."

Then he explained that his brother-in-law Xacinto had found that umbrella in a field in Friol and it had looked like a good umbrella to him and since it was lost, he'd taken it, mainly because it started raining hard at that very moment. Xacinto opened the umbrella and it went and swallowed him. Exactly like I'm telling you: it swallowed him. It was open and went flying through the air to the threshing floor of his family home, next to the hayloft. Xacinto, who was inside the umbrella, was shouting through the mouth on the handle. His wife, his in-laws and brothers- and sisters-in-law came running.

"It's Xacinto!" he told his wife.

"If you really are Jacinto Onega Ribas, who's married to María García Verdes, prove it!" she said in Spanish.

And that's when Xacinto stuck out his tongue for the first time.

"That's his tongue!" said his wife.

And it was true, because Xacinto had a really long tongue that hung out of his mouth, something that earned him a lot of arrests when he did his military service in Zamora 8. And now, since he'd become an umbrella, it'd grown even more with the exercise he got sticking it out to show he was there and with the way he'd caress his family members and even the cows, because the only way he could eat was to suckle.

"Why don't you take him to the fairs?" asked Guerreiro, regretting having given him a peseta when Xacinto's brother-in-law showed him the cap.

"My sister won't let me. She even sleeps with the umbrella! After all it is her husband!"

The man announced he was going off to rest and said goodbye to Guerreiro, who continued along his way. The little man continued talking with the umbrella. The umbrella must have said something to him that he didn't like, because Guerreiro clearly saw the man hit it. The umbrella screamed a bit. It was raining up there in Arís, along the side of the dark Arneiro. Before he started down the hill to Lombadas, Guerreiro mounted some crags and saw how the man opened the umbrella with great effort and got underneath it. Soon the umbrella started to fly just over the ground, over the flowering *xesta* bushes. It flew against the wind and you could see the man hanging at the end of the handle. And then Guerreiro went and shouted with all his might:

"Mr Xacinto!"

The umbrella took a great leap and kept on going. Guerreiro insists it was headed to Guitiriz and after that to Coruña.

Figueiras of Bouzal

Figueiras lived in Bouzal, at the foot of the sierra, where the oak trees are so lovely. He was a short, chubby fellow, very dark, with snapping eyes and a nose like that of the fellows in the Prophets, out of proportion and hooked on that face that was as round as a ball. He was quite the plaintiff, dreamer of indictments, and spent his life going from lawyer to lawyer, left farming and spent his own money and a good part of his wife's and when he died, he was in court, trying to have a bachelor brother's testament nullified because he'd left his property to a woman who owned a tavern in Castro, the widow of a Maragato. One day Figueiras fell ill and died in a few hours, during which time he had few lucid moments and was mostly delirious, reciting the negative decisions he'd received during his career as a litigant, which he knew by heart. In a moment when he felt some relief from that sudden fever and the pain in his side, he asked his wife to put a Civil Code he had that once belonged to a court clerk from Bretoña and a statement from a lawyer in Coruña regarding the aforementioned invalidity of his brother's will in the casket because he was surely going to die.

"You continue the case, my dear Gumersinda, and I'll send you some more information from wherever I happen to be!"

Figueiras died and went to the other world with the Civil Code in the pocket of his new jacket and between its pages the statement from the lawyer in Coruña, which was in his favor. A month later, at the advice of a neighbor, Gumersinda went to visit the tavern owner. She was a pleasant woman, very fair-skinned, with curves, smiling, fond of anisette, very attractive considering she was forty, who in order to avoid, some said, the shame of a court case and having to show letters in which Figueiras' brother, Xosé Pértega López – that was his name – asked for her hand in marriage, gave Gumersinda five thousand pesetas and a sow of good stock that was expecting. The truth is the Maragato's widow had suitors who were keen to marry her and she hoped to wed and it wasn't to her advantage to be involved in such matters.

Gumersinda went back to Bouzal with the money inside her blouse, calmly prodding the pig, humming softly, since Figueiras had been in the ground for barely four weeks, and burping from the anisette the Maragato's widow had invited her to drink. With the going price of hogs that year, she calculated if the pig had eight piglets, that would mean such and such a profit and she could buy another sow and start raising them and from reales that were worth a quarter of a peseta she went on to counting pesos, going over the famous lists of figures like the milkmaid in the fable. In the space of a quarter of a league, she figured out all the money she had in her noggin and was so surprised she let out a whistle. Then a crow who was perched on the gate to a field spoke to her:

"What have you done, Gumersinda?"

It was Figueiras himself, the bird's head high like her husband used to hold it when he was angry and its beak as sharp as his nose had been.

"A person has to eat every day!" responded the widow, starting to cry.

"Enemies in my own house!" screamed the crow, that is Figueiras.

It then fell flat on the road, next to a puddle. Gumersinda looked at it, not knowing what to do. After all it was Manuel, Figueiras, her husband. Slowly she went over to the cadaver.

The crow, its feet sticking up in the air, didn't move. The pig snuffled around it. It was dead. Gumersinda had to get hold of the sow, who was going to sink her teeth into the body. She took off her apron and wrapped her husband up in it. She kept on walking, thinking about what she would do with those mortal remains. When she got them home, she lit a small lamp next to the bird's head. Maybe it would be a good idea to inform the neighbors and hold a wake or something, but she didn't dare. Before dawn she put the crow in a box of Astorga muffins and went to bury it in a secluded spot in the cemetery at Seixo. And Figueiras was lucky because, before Gumersinda put him in the box, she wrapped him in newspapers that contained the basis for the codification of the Galician Provincial Laws. Things like that happen. Now Figueiras has something to spend his time on, if he's still an expert in matters of law. The cemetery of Seixo is behind the church, on the southern side of the hill, and there's a big old yew tree growing there, whose roots and shade are shared equally among all the faithful dead.

The Secret Don José

One Delfín of Mocende went to wait for the car that was going to take him to Mondoñedo from his native Bretoña when in the place they call Castro do Vento he saw a tailor in a field. There he was with his table, cutting. The tailor was small and pot-bellied and wearing a red cap. He was cutting a yellow piece of fabric.

"Good day, God be willing!" Delfín greeted him.

"My name is Don José!" answered the tailor in Spanish.

"Well, good day, Don José!" repeated Delfín.

And as soon as he'd said it, the tailor and his table disappeared, as did his scissors and the yellow cloth. It was as if the earth had swallowed him up. Nobody believed this had happened when Delfín told the story, so he got hopping mad and stopped saying hello to the disbelievers. The tailor had appeared less than ten yards away from him and the first thing Delfín saw were the scissors gleaming in the sun. They were strange scissors, ones like he'd never seen, made of two identical sickles. The tailor's cap looked rather like the miter of a bishop. You could even prove in court that the tailor was small because his head didn't reach as high as the table. The grass covered his feet, but Delfín remembered that they'd looked like goat's hooves, although he couldn't swear to it. Mulling this over, Delfín decided that the tailor definitely wasn't from around those parts, maybe he wasn't even a regular human being, but instead belonged to the ancient family in the prehistoric *castro* and was a tailor to the Moors or Celts. Delfín thought more about Don José. He was proud and vain and wanted to be called Don José, which might be his real name, but perhaps he was forbidden to use the "Don" with it and when he heard somebody else say it, he had no choice but to run off. And he wouldn't work as a tailor for himself, it'd have to be for somebody else. And who would that somebody else be who was going to wear yellow? You don't see people around these parts wearing yellow, not even in the fairs at Monterroso or Vilalba. And were there looms down around there?

The smartest thing, in Delfín's opinion, was to think that Don José and the other fellow, the one who's going to wear the yellow clothing, are keeping watch over something around there, a treasure to be precise. If he runs into the tailor again, Delfín's not going to call him Don José, because he'll just run away, so instead he'll call him Don Antón and ask him about the treasure because there must be one, it's easy money. He told the priest at Bretoña and the priest told him that, even if he did find a treasure, it'd be worth next to nothing because the government had the habit of keeping everything.

Delfín was a friend of mine and came to visit one Thursday during the Corpus.

"I dreamed there was a gold pot on the fire, sitting on a silver trivet, and they threw in a white chicken to cook and the pot ate the chicken and spat out the bones. Then the government came and took the pot and trivet and left me only the chicken bones. Is that fair, do you think?"

"And what did the government look like?" I asked him.

Delfín looks at me and sees I believe everything he's telling me and I'm not laughing at him. Delfín reckons I'm as spiritual and intellectual as he is, I bet.

"The government was a hat, a very big hat. It opened its mouth and gobbled up everything. Then it spat out the bones of the white chicken and a black chicken, which I hadn't noticed. I looked and it had no egg. The government, I mean the hat, was going along, playing the pot like a drum, heading up through the forest by Rioseco."

Delfín shakes his head, takes a blue cloth from his pants pocket and wipes his mouth. And in Spanish, beating on the table, he says to me:

"It's just not worth finding treasures!"

Rello of Pontemil

Rello was a quiet fellow. He would sit in a corner of the tavern, watching the card games people were betting on and sipping his mug of red wine from San Fiz. His dog Listo was as quiet and silent as he was. It would rest its head on its master's leg and doze, its long ears falling over its eyes. Rello never talked about anything. When a card game was over, he would go and sit down where there was another one. If they asked him why he didn't play, he said he didn't know how to bet.

"I always go too high!" he insisted.

At exactly midnight on Saturday night, Rello would retire and his Listo would follow him out, wagging its tail. Rello always took a newspaper from the tavern with him, mostly an old one, other times with pages missing. Rello hardly knew how to read or couldn't read at all, but the newspaper was his eternal companion. A fellow named Rozas, who liked to argue and was quite curious and explained what they said in Madrid when Joselito the bullfighter died, asked him one night why he took *El Debate*. Rello turned red and said that it was always a good thing to have a newspaper around the house. Weeks later, from a nephew of his, Rozas heard that at the end of the day Rello would sit on the balcony of his house, which looks out over the river, with the newspaper open in front of him as if he were reading and he'd spend a good hour or so there. Since I got along well with Rello, I asked him why he did that.

"You won't tell a soul?"

"Why, of course not!"

Rello had run into a certain Xestoso of Montes on the

road to Pontemil one night as it was growing dark. The road to Pontemil goes down to the river through an oak grove they call A Adrela and when it reaches the bottom, it runs through a lot, which is usually a mud flat, with a dozen old chestnut trees and a few alders. Xestoso of Montes died some while back, twelve or fifteen years ago. He was very learned in international politics, knew about the loss of Cuba and when the War of 1914 began, he bought *La Esfera* so he could collect Matania's drawings of battles, which he used to decorate his house. In the other world he must have continued to be concerned about the matters of this one because what he wanted to find out from Rello, which is why he'd appeared to him and scared him silly, was if the Kaiser had gone back to ruling in Berlin. Rello was afraid to admit to Xestoso that he didn't know how to read the paper and didn't know who the Kaiser was when Xestoso offered him two pesos a week if he'd keep an eye on things in the newspapers, in case the Kaiser returned. So Xestoso could see him reading the newspaper, Rello would sit on the sunny balcony.

"Xestoso pays very punctually," Rello assured me.

And after thinking about it a bit, scratching his head with his right hand while he lifted his old hat with the left and whispering in my ear, he asked me:

"And did the Kaiser return?"

I explained to him who Kaiser Wilhelm II was, with his moustache and shrunken arm, how he'd fled from Germany, gone to live in Holland in a place where the finest apples grew and there was lots of cheese, how he'd got married a second time, to a blond, chubby woman, and set up a farm.

"And is he still alive?"

I didn't want to tell him a lie and told him the Kaiser had died. I realized this meant posing a moral question for Rello. If the Kaiser were dead, he couldn't return to Berlin and it was deceptive not to tell Xestoso of Montes the truth. Rello went along the road to A Adrela, thinking. A little while later I ran into him in the tavern at Empalme. He was standing over by the kegs of wine. He was about to leave, followed as always by Listo. On top of the wine barrel was the newspaper. He took it, folded it, made a kind of sign to me by slightly bowing his head and left without even saying good night. I realized that he was still collecting two pesos a week from Xestoso – may he rest in peace – to keep an eye out for the Kaiser, in case he ever returned.

The Moor's Jacket

Felipe of Francos had a girlfriend in Ribeira de Piquín, near Meira in the Lugo area, and would go to see her, seated on his mule, a tall, spotted mule with its ears perked up, its tail braided and a solemn, regular gait. Meira was always famous as a mule-producing area and all the ones ridden by the Holy Cistercian Order in the Spanish Empire came from the Royal Abbey. There are none better in Tortosa, or Poitou in France. In Meira the Catalonian stud, because it's a serious breed, was always prized. Felipe, as I said, was riding his mule and when he reached Vilares, which is just a couple of mills, left the mule in the shed of Porteiro of Beza, a good friend of his, and continued on foot to the girl's house, where, as the song goes, the door would be:

... closed
with a blade of straw.

Felipe was, and is, tall, skinny, pale, and has a moustache. There are a lot of pale-skinned persons around there, kind of dark, sometimes swarthy like gypsies. Perhaps families arrived there from far away or they're mixed with the Baluros, that strange Terra Chá tribe people don't know much about. On one of his amorous trips, Felipe met a man digging with a hoe in the middle of the road. He didn't look familiar and even his clothing didn't seem to be from those parts. He was wearing a red cap with a green pompon and for pants he wore large, yellow bloomers. It was late afternoon.

"Did you lose something?" Felipe asked him from atop his mule.

"My jacket," the stranger said.

Felipe spent half an hour watching how the man he didn't know dug and dug and he did it very well and quickly, so he soon had a hole that he fit in, since he was short-legged and had something of a hump on his back. He got into the hole, then came out of it with a jacket made all out of gold.

"What, made of gold!" I said to Felipe.

"Yes, sir, gold!"

The little fellow put the jacket on and buttoned it up. Once he had it on, he beat on his chest with both fists and it sounded like metal.

"What's so special about you?" Felipe asked him, taking off his hat.

"Can't you see I'm a Moor?" said the fellow with the gold jacket.

And he told Felipe that, traveling during the cool part of the day, he'd sat down to take a nap over by Xunqueiras, also so he wouldn't have to go through the Lodoso neighborhood during the day, because he didn't want to be seen wearing those clothes. Then, after he'd set his jacket on the ground, by its own weight it kept sinking down until it was buried in the soft earth of the riverbank and it wasn't just because of the weight, but because, being made of gold that had come from hidden treasures, it liked to be underground and liked to hide so its owner would wonder where it had gone to. What's more, the jacket had the bad habit, when it went burrowing, of looking for the best road to go to a bridge and then it would stay there, making a comfortable cave and spending centuries without moving.

"That's why I always travel with a pick or hoe or shovel, because not a day goes by but I have to look for it."

"That's lot of work!"

"But there's no other clothing as elegant as this jacket!"

The Moor asked Felipe if he wanted to try it on and Felipe

said yes and put on the jacket, which was tight on him and very heavy. As soon as Felipe had it on, it began to move back and forth and pull Felipe toward the ground so strongly and insistently that it knocked him over. When Felipe fell, the jacket wanted to go on into the earth and Felipe was already half buried alive when the Moor lent him a hand.

"Hold on, Felipe, my boy!" he said to him.

And putting the jacket on again, the Moor went skipping along the road to Lodoso. The jacket gleamed with the last rays of sun on that soft September afternoon.

Polido of Sabuceira

Polido was accused of murdering a trader called Gareto, a small fellow with a pock-marked face, who was always ticked off and yelling in Spanish. Gareto, who was from Cacabelos, had cheated Polido on the sale of a cow that turned out to have consumption and Polido swore that he was going to blow his head off the first time he ran into him on one of the paths. Gareto turned up on the bridge at Beces with a bullet hole in his neck. In the inside pocket of his black corduroy vest he had twelve thousand pesetas and, according to the word around the country fairs, a love letter from a woman who had an inn in Lugo. Polido had witnesses that said he'd been in Meira the day of Gareto's death, at a funeral and also in the tavern, enjoying a stew and playing Briscola. But people didn't really believe him, especially because the murder wasn't done to rob him. Polido was a great one to go around at night. He'd run into a wolf in O Marco, say something to it and the wolf would run away. One day at the fair in Monte he saw a guy arrive wearing a white hat and using a cane with an antler handle. Polido circled around him two or three times and then went to talk to Corporal Santomé:

"That fellow's passing counterfeit money."

Corporal Santomé searched the fellow in the Panama hat and found twenty home-made pesos on him. The Corporal asked Polido how he knew about it.

"He smelled like lead!" was the response.

Polido cured his gas with a secret herb, was an expert at putting rings in the snouts of truffle-hunting pigs, made shaving brushes from badger hair, blew cigarette smoke out of his ears to amuse children, shaved cadavers, dealt in gold mines and insisted that, when he worked as a watchmaker in New Orleans, he'd stayed in the executioner's house.

Polido was already fifty years old when he decided to get married. He found a girl he liked in Couto Cachín. She was forty, fair-skinned, youthful and healthy as a cow. Polido owned some fields in Sabuceira and had half of the Polido family's house in Abertosa. In May the cherry trees are so full of blossoms you can't see the house. On the side that looks up the hill is the oak grove in Rodil. Polido explained to me that Carlos III had it planted so he could make ships in Ferrol out of the wood. Carlos III, who according to Polido was a king who paid attention to detail, ordered a report on the prevailing winds, the moisture in the atmosphere and the type of terrain. But, getting back to Polido's wedding, the seamstress from Couto Cachín begged him to swear he hadn't had anything to do with Gareto's death, either in thought or word or deed. Polido promised to swear it before they went to church. The seamstress was very much in love and embroidered handkerchiefs for Polido and put initials on his underwear, the likes of which had only ever been seen in the Balmonte family, who were my relatives.

"She made him a nightshirt," one of his nephews said, "so he could wear it when he had guests, around the feast of St Marina."

One day, when he was getting the paperwork taken care of and buying a dining-room set, on the way back to the village from Vilalba, Polido and the seamstress crossed the bridge at Beces.

"Here's where it happened!" said Polido, recalling Gareto's death.

And then he pointed his finger at the place where the cadaver had appeared. And the seamstress told everybody: three dark stains on the wall turned into blood, as if it had just been shed. They were bloodstains and it was Gareto's blood.

Nobody could get it out of the seamstress' head. No matter how much Polido swore he was innocent, the seamstress stood firm and refused to marry him. She cried, she really did, and lost eight kilos. And Polido, who was really upset, shut himself up in the house. If anybody went by, he'd close the shutters. He started drinking corn liquor and listening to "The Siege of Zaragoza" on the phonograph he'd brought back from America.

Soleiro in the Form of a Crow

These stories about talking crows or people who reappear from their fields in the other world in the form of a crow should all be put together in one place, but they're scattered throughout this book, here and there.

Years ago, around the start of autumn, I sat at the same table in a bar in Lugo as an old geezer I knew, who lived in the Portes neighborhood in Terra Chá. I asked my friend what was new around Azúmara.

"Do you know that fellow Soleiro?"

"A lame guy who'd go around *quendas* time, at the beginning of the month, to Mondoñedo?"

"That's him. Well, he appeared to his wife in the form of a crow."

Soleiro would set up in the village square, under the stone columns they call the Sombreireiro Arches, and sell wool, giving good weights to customers, using a hand-held scale. Yes, I remembered him well. Like me, he was a customer at Pallarego's barbershop. He took advantage of the *quendas* – the calends in May – to get his hair cut. He was a taciturn fellow, a heavy smoker, and stuttered. He never liked the prices and it was hard for him to get the *l* in the word "lower" right.

"Are you sure it was him? He said l-l-l-l-lower?"

"Yep, he did, sir. As a crow he stuttered just like he did when he was a man!"

His wife was returning home from a house in Monte, where she'd gone to sell some chickens. On her head was the empty basket she'd used to transport them that morning. She felt something land inside it. She took the basket down and peered inside. A crow had lighted on an apron in which she'd wrapped a loaf of bread she'd gotten in Mondoñedo. The woman recognized the dead man right away because of the way it talked and coughed.

"Soleiro always smelled like smoke."

"So did the crow."

It told the woman to keep walking. So the woman covered it with a bit of paper to keep it from getting wet.

Soleiro had come from the other world to advise his widow not to sell some land she had over in Castro. That's what she said, although the neighbors said the crow mostly insisted that the widow shouldn't remarry and should send a nephew who worked in the house off to Venezuela. The woman really wanted to know where the crow was staying, but it wouldn't tell her anything about that. When she got to Portes, the crow flew out from under *El Progreso*, the newspaper that was covering it, to the roof of the *cabozo*, where they stored the corn. The widow shouted to see if it wanted anything for supper, but the crow wouldn't answer. Maybe it wanted porridge and got stuck on the letter *p*, which gave it as much of a problem as the letter *m*. Even though the visit had its effect on the widow, she was still inclined to sell the fields. That's what she told the crow, who stood there, not saying anything, and disappeared into the night with the windstorm. But then it returned. It pecked on the window-pane of the bedroom and even aimed at the widow's eyes. It was speaking now.

"Don't sell, don't sell, damn it all!"

The neighbors heard it scream with a human voice. This went on for a week. Since the widow had been thoroughly frightened, was jumpy, had visions and couldn't sleep, she went to a famous medicine man in Vilalba named Pita of San Cobade.

"And what did Pita prescribe for the widow Soleiro?"

"A purgative, I think. And he ordered her to write on a hundred sheets of paper: 'I will not sell. Signed: Me, Josefa Ribas.' She was supposed then to drop the papers along all the paths. It took her a month to write them and scatter the papers around the crossroads and bridges."

My friend showed me one of the pieces of paper, which he'd found at the junction in Moncelos. The paper flew about here and there, waiting for Soleiro to return in the form of a crow and read it.

When Penedo Went Hunting

Penedo of Oirán bought a second-hand shotgun and headed for the woods, a novice hunter at the age of fifty. He had very good eyesight, which he thought was the most important thing you needed to triumph in deer hunting. A teacher from Salamanca assigned to Oirán showed him a thing or two. One day Penedo got up early and went to the woods by Pereiro to hunt from a blind. He sat down, half hidden in a clump of thorny *xesta* bushes, his shotgun ready. He didn't move for an hour, waiting, and nothing went by. That can't have been like hunting in Salamanca. He didn't smoke, he didn't move, he didn't whistle. And there he was, sitting quietly, not moving an inch, another hour when a magpie came and perched on the barrel of the shotgun. Penedo didn't move. The magpie walked up and down the barrel, cleaned its beak, stretched, spreading wide its wings, opened and closed its long tail seven times in a row and sat down facing Penedo. This is what Penedo says: it sat down. Penedo couldn't shoot at it because the magpie was sitting on the barrel. He could scare it off, but that would also frighten all the game that might be in the area. The magpie looked at Penedo, stared right into the hunter's eyes. Penedo started getting dizzy, looking at its nervous pupils, golden, then black, then red. Finally the magpie spoke:

"This isn't the time, my friend!"

Penedo didn't know what to say. The magpie scratched the barrel with its beak again, then jumped onto Penedo's old beret and flew off. Penedo gave up hunting, fired a few shots into the air so the teacher could hear him and went back to Oirán. He decided to return to the woods with two shotguns, one he'd borrow from the priest, and when the magpie came back and perched on one of the barrels, Penedo would shoot at him with the other. It didn't matter if the magpie were the soul of the Widower of Couzán, who'd been a great hunter and when he was alive, got really mad when he found other hunters in the woods. He went around alone with his dogs Prim and Prats. His dogs were always called that. He was probably upset that Penedo had become famous! Penedo returned to the woods with his two shotguns and placed himself where he'd been the previous time. A little over half an hour later the magpie appeared, but it didn't perch on either of the shotguns and settled instead on Penedo's old beret.

"Don't play tricks on me, Penedo, my boy. I'm not poor!"

Penedo rested the shotguns on the ground. The magpie went down and sat on one of them.

"Unless I turn into a rabbit!" said the bird.

Penedo untied the package where he had his snack and gave the magpie a nibble of cheese. And while he was offering it something to eat, he spoke to it in Spanish, trying to convince it to turn into a rabbit.

"Just for the fun of seeing the change, woman!"

And if it did become a rabbit, it should go over there, where the blue flax blooms around Midsummer's Eve, so he could test his eyesight. The magpie, having eaten its fill of cheese, said all right, jumping in front of Penedo, spinning on its left foot, and in a jiffy it turned into a rabbit, running leisurely toward the fields of flax. Penedo says he took both shotguns and fired all four shots at the same time. The rabbit hopped abruptly and fell down dead. Penedo went to retrieve the body and discovered it was just a skin. A dry skin, held together by a rubber band. Penedo took off the rubber band and some papers fell out. Yes, it belonged to the Widower of Couzán. There were some letters, a promissory note, a doctor's prescription and the bill for the burial, including the casket and music from Mondoñedo. The widower had written at the bottom of the bill: "Seems like a lot to me!" He must have written it after he died. Penedo took the skin and papers to one of the widower's nieces. The niece went to see a lawyer in Lugo and cashed in the promissory note. The priest at Oirán didn't mind putting the rabbit skin in the widower's niche. And Penedo sold the shotgun to a fellow from Ferreira and next time the Devil could go hunting.

Merlo of Lousadela

Lousadela is in Invernegas de Montes, where the Eirelle ravine opens onto a green meadowland on a hillside, where more than a dozen streams descending from the dark Arnaceira mountains flow into the river. It gets its name from a quarry that gives blue slate in large, even slabs. The land is poor. People make a living from having livestock in the hills, a ragged set of animals with coarse hair that wander free from April to October, and they take their sheep, so they say around there, *a quendas* or monthly, since each month a different household oversees the minor tasks. They harvested only a few, low-quality potatoes, a bit of rye in the untilled areas and clearings, there are very good turnip greens in season, bitter, and in all of Lousadela only one fruit tree to be seen: the cherry tree in the courtyard of St Margaret's church. The people from around there are tall, blond, thin, taciturn. The only smiling face in those lonely parts was my friend Merlo, who was a hunter, clog-maker, fisherman, watch repairman in the winter, gelder and bagpipe musician. He had two jackets, gaucho's spurs made of silver and a gold tooth. He came back from Buenos Aires speaking a bit of Italian and the widower, they said, of a woman from Málaga. He had two dogs, a pointer and a setter from Burgos, who came when he called to them in Italian. Merlo's Italian was like a song. In the tavern by the bridge, once the people gathered there had had a little to drink, they would ask Merlo to talk to them. My friend Merlo would then get up on a stool or rest on the crates of herring and deliver the speech he himself called "the Sermon of the Two Flags," which he'd heard given by the Ambassador of

Italy in Argentina at the inauguration of some Don Galileo schools. What with the twenty words in Italian Merlo really knew and a thousand more he made up, my friend was a splendid orator, using plenty of gestures, opening wide his arms. Even though he was a Maragato, the tavern owner, Mariano Nistal, always ended up in tears because he was moved by the pathetic eloquence. Then, so sales wouldn't suffer, Nistal's wife, Miz Basilia, would come to collect for the drinks because her husband, overcome with emotion, got the charges mixed up. When he finished his sermon, Merlo would pull two little flags out of his jacket pocket, an Italian one and an Argentinian one, and the audience would applaud. I sat in the front row, next to a barrel of Valdeorras wine.

In wintertime, Merlo would leave Lousadela and go around the nearby villages, fixing watches. Most Sundays he'd go down to the Melles' big house and let people know he was coming and the people who lived there would sit on the steps or in the archways to listen to one of Merlo's speeches. When he finished, he'd imitate birds and swallow a lighter that wasn't lit, then take it out lit from behind his right ear. Some were unwilling to believe it and stared at Merlo's ear, which was all singed.

"This is Greek science, Father," he assured the priest at Pacios.

"You didn't fraternize with the Devil in Buenos Aires, Simon the Magician?" the priest asked him.

And Don Xosé Rodríguez Mariñán would go and spit in his ear. People would laugh. But once the priest spat and smoke came out of Merlo's ear and you could hear the same sound red-hot iron makes when it's forged and dipped in the water. The women screamed, the children were frightened, the men looked at one another and the priest took a step backward.

I didn't see this with my own eyes and I'm sorry I didn't. I won't see it now because Merlo died a short while ago from a cold spot he got in his liver. They buried him with his new jacket and if they didn't take the little flags out of the pockets, they're still with him. It was snowing the day he was buried in Invernegas de Montes, the birch trees were bare and all the birds he'd imitated were gone, titmice, finches, quails and even the *merlo*, the blackbird Merlo had gotten his nickname from.

Carrexo of Fontes

Fontes is a small place, four white houses, way back in Ribeira de Piquín, in the old Cistercian lands of Meira. All the chestnut trees there died from the worm called the *tinta*, but there are still some lovely oak groves, at Sanxeés and Pousada, and good fields, fallow lands and, next to the mud flats, where the woodcock flies in wintertime, there are alders, birches and willows. Fontes is a good name, there being several good springs with a lot of water flowing in a thin, cool stream they call the Friars', falling from a high iron pipe. In season the banks are clad in purple foxglove. In the house facing the old road, crowned by a wide, square chimney covering half the roof, lived Carrexo, also known as Antón of Xil. Carrexo was small and dark, bald on the back of his head, with very lively, little black eyes, forever shifting, unable to remain still, unable to sit down for five minutes. Carrexo returned from Buenos Aires, where he'd worked as a butcher, because of the full moon there. The moon in Buenos Aires, according to Carrexo, is very heavy. My friend and countryman could never understand how it was people failed to notice. Carrexo, in order to walk about the streets at night, would stick a piece of wood under his beret or hat and because he lived on the top floor of a house, he could hear the creaking of the beams that supported the roof.

"I can tell you they'd give a bit with the scent of the full moon!"

But when Carrexo returned, he was sensitive to moonlight and never at ease in Fontes either. He reinforced the beams in his house, put supports in the attic and his bedroom and made himself a cap out of oak. Later, in a circus in Lugo, around St Froilan, he bought a French military helmet from the War of 1914 from a clown for fifty pesos. In any event, not wanting to challenge the moon, when it was full-moon time, he would get into bed, put on the helmet and open an umbrella. But by giving the matter a lot of thought, he discovered that he could ward off the moon's force by putting a round mirror they made him in *Vidreira Lucense* on the roof, directly above his bedroom. That way he could send back to the moon what he called "uneven rays," only he knows why.

Carrexo continued studying the matter and arrived at the conclusion that, if he wore some kind of light on his head, he could go out at night and not suffer any harm on the days of the new moon. He prepared a hat with a lantern and with that apparatus on his head he'd go down to the tavern in Pousada to play card games for wagers. But from his days in Buenos Aires he was left with headaches he called "visions," not very accurately, because in fact they were noises like those of a mouse in the attic. Carrexo confessed to me once, in a fair at Augaxosa, that he was afraid of going crazy. His sister wanted him to go to Santiago so Dr Somoza could take a look at him.

"Well, he belongs to the Pedro of Sarria group, you know, and you can trust them!" I said encouragingly. But Carrexo insisted he could manage by himself. He maintained that the crux of the argument was in staying awake for a hundred hours straight so the visions, that is to say the noises, that came to him as soon as he fell asleep would be unable to do their work and get bored and leave. But the noises never got bored, they grew and finally they continued working when Carrexo was awake. He decided to drown them and stuck his head in a pail of water. But the one who drowned was stubborn, old Carrexo. He could write well, with nice, rounded handwriting, all neatly arranged. He had a thing about accents, like Radiguet as a child, and put one or sometimes two on every syllable.

I never saw so many dry leaves on a road as there were on the one from Fontes to Meira, passing alongside the oak grove at Pousada. If the wind's blowing, you can hear the leaves swirl a thousand feet away.

Leiras of Parada

The day after the feast of St Martin, my friend Leiras of Parada, a serious fellow with a moustache, puts the capons in their cage for the second and last fattening-up period. And even though the residents of the capon cage in Terra Chá, fed as required, unable to move, soaking up the heat from the kitchen stove, already sleep well, the good capon farmers give them a little something extra once or twice a day, after the ground meat bits, half a glass of sweet wine. Wine from Getafe, they call it around there. Leiras of Parada cared for his capons, like I said. Some of them will go to the fair in Vilalba and others will go toward paying the bills. These latter are called "bill capons" and, to help them drop off, he sits in a rocking chair that once belonged to the sister of a priest in Goiriz and starts snoring. Most of the time he ends up dropping off at the same time as the capons, who are addled, their heads drooping. And Leiras explains to me that, when he used to see well, thanks to some glasses Gasalla of Lugo prescribed for him when he was a witness at a hearing, before he nodded off, he would read the capons a chapter from a book such as *Bertoldo, Bertoldino and Cascacenno* or Amor Meilán's *A History of the Province of Lugo* or a newspaper article. Leiras tells me I'm not going to believe what he's about to tell me. He strokes his moustache, smiles, twists the cap he's wearing around his head, scratches his cheek for a few moments and smiles again:

"Yes, my friend, they liked *Bertoldo* and wouldn't go to sleep."

"And do you think they understood any of it?"

"I'm saying they wouldn't go to sleep listening to *Bertoldo*, that's all. One day Cruces the town councilor, you remember him, gave me a newspaper from Madrid so I could read an article by a fellow named Zozaya. I read it aloud in front of the capons. That was exactly what they needed. What a waste of ink! They fell right asleep, my friend!"

Leiras of Parada gets up, goes to the drawer of the sideboard and takes out an envelope with an issue of *La Libertad*, Madrid, dated March 6th, 1932, with an article by Mr Antonio Zozaya titled "The Untarnished Victory." Half a page, in fine print.

"It's better than two blankets and half a bottle of Tres Cepas cognac!"

There are always twenty-two capons in the cages, in that kitchen with the dirt floor, silent and bored. The day of the fair at Vilalba they'll be there, soft yellow, stiff from the frosty air, sitting on white cloths, in Santa María Square.

Louredo of Hostes

I met Louredo, like I met so many others, in my friend
Pallarego's barbershop. I could tell a lot of things about
Louredo, but what I want to talk about here is the case of
his glasses bought in Valencia, in the square or street of
Jaime I. The thing was that Louredo never dreamed. He
was doing his military service in the cavalry regiment of
Queen Victoria Eugenia and had a sergeant who called the
squadron together every morning and told the soldiers what
he'd dreamed the night before. How that guy could dream!
Most of the time he'd dream about a trip to the Philippines
or that he'd won the lottery and left the army to go to Madrid
and was sitting in a theater. And he told the plot of the play
they were performing with a lot of attractive actresses and
before the curtain fell, they'd call him up on stage and he'd
go in dress uniform with his helmet and take the lead actress
to the baths at Archena, where he was from. Louredo was sad
that he couldn't dream either about his village or about the
procession to St Marina's shrine. Being of medium height,
with bowed legs and a spotted eye, he would have liked to
dream that he was tall and a leggy, pale-skinned, dark-eyed
girl from Valencia was mad about him and would sit still like
a hen does and Louredo would stroke her softly. Louredo,
who was very respectful, went to see Sergeant Granero:

"Excuse me, sergeant, sir. What does one have to do in
order to dream?"

"Buy yourself some glasses, Galician!" he answered,
laughing at him.

Louredo took the answer seriously and didn't stop until
he found a person in Valencia who was willing to sell him

some glasses so he could dream, glasses that according to Louredo were dark with a silver frame. The first night he went to sleep with them on, he dreamed an entire movie, but it went so fast he couldn't understand the plot. The only thing he recalled afterward was that he was leaving when it was over and a fat lady gave him a coffee-and-milk-flavored candy.

"Was she pretty or ugly?" I asked him.

"Well, considering it was the first time I dreamed about a woman, she turned out pretty decent and was wearing a red blouse."

Since then, as long as he went to bed with the glasses on, Loureiro always dreamed about huge triumphs, about a little lady who danced or a black woman who had a canary in a cage and how they gave him the best horse in the whole regiment. Everything was fine, except when he had watermelon for supper and then he dreamed that he was climbing up on a roof and they pushed him off. He died a bachelor and bequeathed his glasses to his nephews so they could take turns dreaming. The nephews laughed at their uncle and told the local priest in Baroncelle to take the glasses to the rectory. Heaven knows what the Reverend Father Daniel Pernas Nieto dreamed with the aid of the glasses, about fair-skinned Valencian women, red wines, trout banquets, festivities, on those long, cold winter nights, when the birch branches turn ash-gray with frost!

Leiras of Tardiz

His name was Jesualdo Pértega, but he was known as Leiras of Tardiz. His grandfather was Leiras the Elder and his son, Leiriñas. The Tardiz River flows into the Miño from the right-hand side, amid alders and willows, and waters some good fields. All the Leiras of Tardiz were in Buenos Aires, working in bakeries and bread shops. Mr Jesualdo worked in a bakery that belonged to a Lebanese fellow named Monsieur Batani. Old Batani was married to a Greek lady and their son, whose name was Yussef, married a Spanish woman from Málaga, who he soon grew tired of. So he went back home to Lebanon during the vacation, became a Muslim, divorced the woman from Málaga and when he returned to the Plate region, he came with a wife, a German lady, who was very fat, Jewish, and sang on holidays in the Hebrew theater in the Argentinian capital. In one of the works she played the part of Eve. They really applauded her and all the Jews in Buenos Aires said they'd never seen such a good portrayal of Eve, so perfect, with that bluish skin and rocking gait with which she strolled through Paradise. Batani, the father, still cared for the Málaga woman, yet he was also proud of the triumphs of his new daughter-in-law and sent the Málaga lady almond sweets and honey along with pine-nut pastries. I would talk with Leiras in the barbershop about whether Eve had been white or black. Leiras said that, if the Jews applauded Batani's daughter-in-law, they knew exactly what they were doing.

Leiras would tell a lot of stories about Italians and insisted he'd been there for most of them, an eyewitness in the bakery shops of Buenos Aires. For example, an Italian came in wearing a pearly gray Borsalino hat, a green tie and white shoes.

"Could you make me a cake with biscuit, peach jam, whipped cream, trimmed with cherries all around it?"

"Of course!" the employee replied.

"And a braid of toasted almonds to go around the cherries."

"Of course!"

They brought him the cake and the Italian stood there, looking at it, feeling pleased.

"*Bellissima!* And could you put '*E' viva Arnaldino!*' in the middle, with a heart on both sides of each letter?"

"Of course!"

The Italian looked at himself in the mirror, straightened his hat, then pulled up his pants a bit, showing his red socks.

"Here's your cake."

"Could you sprinkle a layer of sugar and cinnamon on top?"

"Of course!"

The employee shows the cake to the Italian.

"Shall I wrap it?"

"Oh no! I'm going to eat it right here!"

The Italian took off his pearl-gray Borsalino, put it on a chair after blowing the seat off, set the cake on top of the candy jars and ate it all up with his fingers.

"And then," Leiras told me, "he asked for two napkins, cleaned himself off, paid and left, bowing to himself in the mirror. What do you think about those people? We Galicians, we're so simple, we just get a package of *petits choux* to take home once in a while on Sunday!"

Muñiz of Parada

I'm sorry the tailor Muñiz of Parada and the parish priest of Vilardelle, Vitorino Graña López, have died because I'd like to give them both a bit of news, completely documented, which would put an end to their differences. Muñiz went to Barcelona to serve the king and, having finished his training, stayed on a couple of years, learning to be a tailor with a fellow named Vinardell, whose shop was next to the cathedral and who was an expert at frock coats and played the violin and pool. This was around 1906. One day like all the rest, in the early afternoon, the valet of the Duke of Tamames came to the tailor shop. His name was Calixto and he explained that his master, who was the most elegant man in Spain in those days, needed four dress jackets in forty-eight hours, since he had to make some social calls and his suitcase had gotten lost in Zaragoza. Vinardell set to work, using the measurements Calixto had given him, and the duke sent notice that he would come by the shop to try the jackets on. Each one had a lining of a different thickness and weight so the duke could use the right one according to the weather. The duke spent six hours at the tailor's and, according to Muñiz, was "extremely finicky" because he kept finding defects. When he got tired of standing, he asked for a basin in which to soak his feet.

Vinardell offered to have him go to his bedroom, but the chamber aide, Calixto, said that dukes were allowed to wash their feet in front of the king. The Duke of Tamames washed his feet right there in the shop, in front of the seamstresses and Muñiz. His feet were so lovely that a buttonhole maker from Murcia confessed she'd fallen in love with the duke and was going to follow him to Madrid. Muñiz of Parada told me all of this while the two of us were sitting in the shade of the apple trees, in the meadow, during the hot days of St Lawrence.

One day a fellow who had six dogs he'd taught to dance nicely arrived at Vinardell's shop. He was looking to get them into the circus, but before that he wanted to dress the doggies up in colored jackets made out of corduroy. So Vinardell could get the clothing right, the owner of the dogs had brought a book in English that explained how to take dogs' measurements when you want to get clothing made for them.

"That book doesn't exist!" said Don Vitorino, the parish priest.

"But I saw it. It had drawings of lots of dogs and a bunch of geometry," insisted Muñiz.

"There's no such thing! And because you're a liar, I'm never going to speak to you again so long as I live!"

Angry, Don Vitorino left, carrying his gray umbrella, taking that lovely little path that goes by Ardeán's field. Muñiz confessed he felt very badly. "Sir, sir, that book really did exist! Dog jackets are complicated due to the curve of the backbone and there was an explanation in the book, using a triangle."

One day Muñiz received word that Don Vitorino was dying in the rectory at Villardelle. Muñiz went to see him.

"I've come to make you believe the story about the book of dog costumes before you die!" Muñiz said to the priest. "Believe me, I swear it on the blessed souls, man!"

"I don't believe you," said Don Vitorino with his last breath.

"My friend, believe me before you die!" Muñiz wept.

"*Non possumus!*"

That is what Don Vitorino Graña López of the Osorio

and Rodil families said and he gave up his soul to God. Muñiz continued to weep. And never again, except to me, did he tell the story of the dog trainer and Vinardell taking the measurements for dogs according to a book written in English. One day, shaking his head, Muñiz told me he no longer knew if he'd dreamed that story about the book.

But that book, written in English, does exist. Its author is a priest, a famous mathematician known as William Oughtred, who lived in the seventeenth century and was such a monarchist he died from glee when he heard the news the Stuarts were being restored to the throne. He is also famous because he was the first to use the Greek letter *pi* to designate the relationship between circumference and diameter and the cross of St Andrew to indicate multiplication. So he wrote a treatise with his own drawings on tailoring for dogs and cats and the procedures for taking their measurements, which many people think is a political satire. I would have liked to tell Don Vitorino Graña about it so he could retract the famous "*Non possumus!*" he shouted out during the last hour of his life to the tailor Muñiz of Parada, who made me a pair of cheap cotton pants with three pockets.

Felipe of Bures

A son of my friend Felipe of Bures has embarked in Vigo for
England. He's going to work as a pot-maker in a workshop in
Wales, where they make big-bellied pitchers. He shows me
this photograph and they have a really fancy handle and are
decorated with little flowers that look like periwinkles. Antón
of Bures has been hired for a good salary. The Bures folks are
quite handy, they're people with a lot of secrets. Felipe went
to work as a stonemason in France when he wasn't much
more than a boy, after the War of 1914 ended, and cut a lot of
stone for the cathedral at Reims, which had been damaged
by German Krupp cannons. He also worked in Amiens.
When he told me about it in Pallarego's barbershop, I gave
him a copy of *The Bible of Amiens* by Ruskin in a Spanish
version published in Valencia. He was the only Lugo native
who worked there, because all the other stonecutters were
from Pontevedra. Felipe was famous for his ability to get
the dust out of the stonecutters' eyes with a hare's whisker,
which is what you're supposed to use. The foreman, a fellow
named Lebrun, a very jovial hunchback according to Felipe,
paid him extra for his work as an eye-doctor. Felipe couldn't
make up his mind if he was going to sleep with the widow
of a sergeant who'd died at the Battle of the Somme. The
widow always wore her husband's medals on her chest. But
he found out in time she had a lot of fake additions, starting
with her dentures.

"And one of her eyes," added Felipe. "I can't recall if it
was the right one or left one. Her round parts as well and her
backside."

When Felipe had had two or three shots of liquor, he

would add false parts, encouraged by my questions: her ears, left foot...

"And I bet she wore a wig," I said to him.

"A red wig, that's right," Felipe confirmed.

We increased the list of fake parts so much that I ended up thinking there'd never been a widow, she was a ghost in human form and her false parts and body shape were hung from that.

Felipe returned from France with a few pesetas, managed to get a stone house and married a neighbor, Andrea, who'd been maid to my relatives, the Montenegros of Begonte. Felipe was the first person who spoke by telephone with Lugo from Paris.

"Was it something urgent?" I asked him when he told me about it.

"Not at all! There was a guy from Betanzos, a real braggart, who said he was going to call Coruña and so I said you could call Lugo too. He said you couldn't. We bet a meal on it. He claimed you couldn't call Lugo because he'd read the telephones in Paris were only for talking with large European cities such as Coruña. Well, I called Lugo, the store *Great Britain*, and ordered some black shoes, size forty-two. And when I got to Lugo two months later, there they were, all nicely wrapped up on a shelf. I paid for them and that was that. The newspaper *El Progreso* published an article about it."

I ask Antón if his father taught him how to get stone dust and other things out of people's eyes with a rabbit's hair. He smiles, opens his wallet and shows me twelve carefully chosen hairs wrapped in cigarette paper.

"There are hares in England too!" I say to him.

"But their whiskers may not be round," he replied.

Perhaps that's true. There must be some difference between a Galician Catholic hare and an Anglican one.

Seixo of Parderrubias

It so happened a fellow named Seixo of Parderrubias saw a small man with an open umbrella, protecting himself from the sun, come out of Abalde field and start walking along the road to Lugo. The road is wide and flat and most of the way passes between idle plots and rye fields. The man's umbrella was huge, measuring about fourteen yards in width. Seixo was heading along the same road and walked faster so he could catch up with the little fellow, because it's always good to share a bit of conversation on a fall morning, when you're on a long trip to see a lawyer. Seixo was a talkative fellow and liked to tell the stories of cases from the beginning, with the settlement in Meira or Cospeito. The little fellow with the umbrella was so small he could pass as a dwarf in a play. Seixo wondered how he could manage such a big umbrella and was ready to advise him that a beret was enough for that light sun on the eve of St Martin. Seixo walked faster, but couldn't catch up to the little guy, who talked constantly and when he came to a muddy spot or a big puddle, would fly over it. He'd fly, yes, sir, and land seven or eight yards beyond it. Seixo ran, but then the other speeded up. Seixo got tired and sat down on a stone wall to roll a cigarette and lost sight of the fellow with the umbrella, who quickly reached the high point at Bexo, which is a hill with birches and a fountain bubbling up beside the road.

Seixo continued on his way and, coming down from Bexo to the river, he saw the man with the umbrella returning. He was going along as fast as when he was heading in the other direction and still had the umbrella open. Seixo did not want to miss the chance to have a conversation with that fellow who wasn't from those parts. He stood right in the center of the road there where it narrows between the rocky crags and took out his tobacco pouch to offer him a smoke. The dwarf came walking up under his umbrella, which didn't weigh a thing, and the little man turned out to be a face, red, round, with a moustache. You could say he didn't have a body because his legs were almost growing out of his neck, two skinny legs they were, ending in iron-trimmed clogs. There was something strange about his face. He had three eyes, believe it or not! Seixo could see them quite clearly. They were big, black eyes. The little guy couldn't get by very well with the umbrella open because Seixo was right smack in the middle of the road, as I said. The little fellow walked right into him, but Seixo didn't move. Actually he couldn't move because he was under the spell of the lights shining from those three eyes. And just when it seemed the little guy was going to run into Seixo, he flew up and over him, disappearing behind the birch trees.

Seixo couldn't believe his eyes and went along, pondering what had happened and if he'd really actually seen the little man or not. Then he ran into Ribalda, a shyster who was advising his opponents in a case about water rights. Ribalda was also a medicine man and could cure bile with seven words.

"And what are you doing around here?" Seixo asked him.

"Doing, I'm not doing a thing. I just happened to be sleeping at Cortón's inn, dreaming about a little man with an umbrella and three eyes. And he went and left my dream and I woke up to see if I could find him. There's nothing that bothers me more than having only half a dream!"

Seixo explained to Ribalda that he'd seen the little man on his way to Lugo and later returning in the direction of Castro.

"He must be going crazy! He didn't give me the chance in my dream to tell him where he was supposed to get the Medina y Marañón book, because I needed to look something up."

Seixo looked at Ribalda for a long time and finally dared to say:

"Against whom?"

Ribalda stroked his long, blond moustache, spat and raised his right hand to his chest:

"Friend, the best thing is for you to settle!"

And Seixo went and settled, although he was losing out according to him. Ribalda received something from both sides: from Seixo, a ham and a leather jacket. He became a friend of Seixo of Parderrubias and made a deal with him, for twelve pesos a year and two cheeses, to dream about the little man with the umbrella because Seixo couldn't sleep, he was so anxious to see the tiny walker with his three wide-open eyes. Ribalda dreamed up the little man for Seixo, who saw him again along the Bexo road, and also dreamed about calves with six legs and two heads and a blue horse that ate with a knife and fork on the pilgrimage to Our Lady of Miracles. Seixo saw everything Ribalda dreamed. It was too bad Seixo had to go to the insane asylum at Conxo on May 7th, 1961, ten years ago now. Ribalda was going to dream up a treasure for Seixo, a treasure with plenty of coins.

"I never touched gold coins, Ribalda!" Seixo said to him.

"Well, you're going to get your fill of them now!" responded Ribalda, charging him two years' dreams up front.

Leiras of Marco

They say Leiras of Marco de Alvare talked with animals, but it isn't true. What is true is that he could understand them and they knew, by some sense that still hasn't been identified, they could come to Leiras in time of need or for some whim they might have. Leiras knew that and tried his best to help them. Once a fellow from Pértega saw a pig on the road to Marco, one of those that are a cross between the native breed and the large white they have around there now. A lovely pig, rather long and low to the ground and light on its feet. It must have already weighed some hundred kilos. It was going along at a good rate, but once in a while would lie down, scratch itself and earn its barley like a donkey. Something was eating at it. The fellow from Pértega, whose name was Mouriz and who is still alive, may he have good health, followed the pig perhaps with the secret hope it would get lost at some crossroads and he could guide the so-easily-found animal to his house. But the pig turned off at the place they call Carreiras and went trotting up to Leiras' house. Mouriz removed his beret and said to himself:

"It's going for advice!"

And so it was. The pig reached Leiras' door, grunted and rooted in the dirt and Leiras came out to greet it. The pig sat down. Leiras looked at it for a while, then, when asked by Mouriz, who'd followed the animal to see how things turned out, told him his client had the turnip-flower itch, which affects certain ladies, and had to avoid scratching itself and the best thing was to give it baths with rye bran and he would give it the first one. And so he did. The pig stood still. When Leiras finished the session, he patted the pig on the back and said to it:

"Go along now back to your sty, slowly, and don't scratch!"

Leiras knew the pig belonged to a neighbor over in Trelle called Novagildo. Well, the fellow's real name was Leovigildo, but his family hadn't understood the priest very well at the baptism and they called him Novagildo. Leiras asked Mouriz to accompany the pig and to relay the prescription to its owner. When Mouriz reached Trelle, which is about half a league away, the pig thanked him.

"Come on, it thanked you?" I asked in surprise.

"Yes, sir, it thanked me!" he nodded while looking at me, "and whenever I went through Trelle, it'd always wave to me from its sty."

Once some Maragatos from over there brought two white hens to Marco, a gift from a cousin in Madrid, the chickens having just arrived from France. They came with a paper that said they would lay two hundred and twelve eggs a year. The rooster, one of those grayish types with white stockings common to that region, didn't want to mate with them. It'd go up to the hens, its head held high, lively, walk around them twice, then leave, disgusted, without trying to mate. They called Leiras, who took a few steps around the threshing floor, followed by the rooster, which kept saying "groló, groló," as if it were confessing to the wise one. Leiras figured out what was going on and went to see Miz Silvina, who was selling codfish for a harvest, and said to her:

"The rooster won't mate with the hens because they're wearing cologne and smell bad to it."

Miz Silvina went out, picked up a hen and sniffed it.

"Hmmm, it's true. They smell like something blue."

Miz Silvina was a rather sad woman, always talking in a romantic way about a miscarriage and a boyfriend she'd had in Monforte.

Leiras washed the hens with vinegar and Seville soap twelve times a day, three days in a row. When he'd finished the treatment, Leiras clapped his hands and the rooster came running and spent the whole morning mating with the chickens.

No dog ever barked at Leiras. They'd come out to the road and keep him company. One day he whistled while beside the river and a snake that was hidden in the grass showed up.

"I wasn't calling you, I was calling Vitorino, who's over there with a goat," Leiras said to the snake.

The snake went back to its nest. Vitorino hadn't heard the whistle, but the goat had and it told its master that Leiras of Marco was calling him.

Leiras was very small, had red hair, one eye was off. He spent most of his time sharpening razors. He found out in a fair at Monte that the Verdes of Sistallo had brought a German shepherd they'd trained at a dog school in Madrid. Leiras went to see it. They became friends. Leiras went for a walk with the dog in the orchard of the stone manor and when he stopped to have a shot at the house of Rei of Corbite, he commented:

"I didn't know you spoke German so well."

They say he died of fright. But that's another story.

Gaito and His Shoe

Manuel the Gaito lost his left foot in Coruña in 1930, when a trolley ran over him. He had in fact just bought a pair of shoes on San Andrés Street. Manuel was in bad shape, especially his mind. He spent hour after hour in bed, thinking about how he was going to walk when he got better and how he'd look as a man with a limp, if a cane would be enough or he'd have to use crutches or they could fit him with a cork foot. After the amputation, he cried a little, but later, angry about his limp, he got really mad and spat on the wall.

"There's no such thing as a good cripple!" he told himself.

When he got over his anger, he'd laugh.

He recovered, but didn't want others to see him walk those first days he was up. In his room he had a cane and crutch and there, with the door closed, he practiced. He tried walking with clogs, with high boots, and ended up trying on the shoes he'd first bought in Coruña. It's important to note he only tried on the right shoe because the stump of his left leg was tucked into a red sock. And while he was walking around his room, he saw to his surprise that the shoe meant for the left foot was starting to move on its own and was walking along beside him as if somebody were wearing it. Gaito studied the shoe very calmly and didn't see anything strange in that. It was an average shoe, like all of them. One day, when Gaito was sitting down, the shoe came out of its place, jumped sideways and clicked its heel a little, like for a dance. It stood first on its heel and next on its toe, jumped from side to side and whirled suddenly, first on the front part, then on its back part. Then it ended with a heel tapping: "tatatatatá tatatá tatá."

"What kind of dance is that?" asked Gaito in a loud voice.

"'O Bom Pequito,' Your Excellency," responded the shoe.

"You dance it very well!"

"Thank you very much," the shoe responded.

It was Portuguese. On the sole, in letters inside a golden circle, was written: "Extra. Ferrer. Alcoy." But from the way it talked it was Lusitanian. Well! Gaito wanted to continue his conversation with the shoe, but it had gone silent. After several days he still couldn't drag a word out of it. He'd walk around his room, the shoe beside him, very quiet. Suddenly Gaito sat down on a chair. The shoe was left alone in the very center of the room and was surprised by the sudden stop.

"Aren't you well?" asked the shoe in Portuguese.

"What's your name?" Gaito took advantage of the opportunity.

"Quinteiro Filho."

And the fellow with the shoe, for it was clear now it wasn't the shoe talking but an invisible person who must have been around a yard and a half tall, told his story. He was a Portuguese who'd been run over by a train in Lugo. He was missing his left foot. When they picked up his remains at the station in Lugo, they were worried because they could only find one of his feet. How were they going to find the other one if it was in a clinic in Rio de Janeiro, embalmed in a glass jar, because it was a very odd foot, with seven toes, two baby ones and the big toe shaped like a pear? Quinteiro Filho, who died in Lugo, remained in the region and, passing by Gaito's house, saw he had an extra shoe. At the same time he'd never been able to wear a shoe on that left foot he'd had, with those deformities, and now it was missing, he found it easy to put on that fine shoe from Alcoy. Gaito and Quinteiro Filho became fast friends. Gaito would go to Lugo and buy shoes, white shoes, sandals, open-cut shoes. And he'd share his pairs with the Portuguese fellow. They'd go out for a walk along the road to Lugo and some even saw the left shoe walking by itself next to Gaito. The priest at Rececende once had to move over on the road to let a white shoe pass that was walking beside Gaito. Standing on its toe, very politely, the shoe bowed and thanked the reverend:

"*Muito obrigado!*"

When Gaito died, the newest left shoe came up to the casket and said in a sad voice:

"Farewell, dear world!" in Portuguese.

With a hop it landed in the casket with the dead man. And they decided to let it.

Pedro Corto

Everyone knew him as Pedro Corto or Pedro Anteiro, but his name was Pedro Regueira García. He was my schoolmate in Riotorto one year there was a typhus outbreak in Mondoñedo and they sent me to the village, to my uncle Serxio Moirón's house. I was eight years old and he was eleven or twelve. He was a slow calligrapher, like the Chinese in the days of the Tang and Song dynasties, and I came to admire him years later. Pedro could do all the Iturzaeta letters on clean sheets of paper. I had really bad handwriting, little mosquitoes squashed every which way on the paper, and I envied Pedro Corto's clear, solemn handwriting learned from José Francisco Iturzaeta's manual, following the Basque tradition of nice handwriting – they served as secretaries to the House of Austria. Cotarelo Mori praised the Iturzaeta handwriting style, as it was called in the required penmanship textbook in the institute in Lugo, where I went to high school. Pedro Corto arrived at school with his big clogs, dressed in a green corduroy jacket that was short on him and narrow and mended pants that covered his knees. He had an enormous scarf with red and purple stripes wrapped around his head, covering his ears. He was very thin, his hair was blond and he had blue eyes like the purest line of the Miranda region. He was always cold and before he copied the lessons, he'd ask the teacher for permission to stick his hands in his pants pockets. He knew how to make paper balloons that would float gaily upward and disappear behind the dark mountains. No matter what direction they went in, even if they headed toward Xudán or the mountains of Asturias or the northeast wind carried them to Meira, Pedro Corto would say:

"Balloons always go toward the sea!"

He'd never seen the sea himself and looked forward to the day when he had to go to Foz, following doctor's orders, with September naps, full of good bacon with fiber and rye bread. But Pedro's talent, his greatest skill, was taming grasshoppers. When the grasshoppers starting coming out in May, Pedro would catch half a dozen of them, put them in a little box with a cover that was half glass and half screen and start taming the restless grasshoppers. It was even harder than the Syrian and Bulgarian art of taming fleas. Pedro Corto's grasshoppers ended up using the swing he put in the box for them and jumping through a double hoop made out of a hairpin and over a hurdle of red paper, like tiny horses. When he turned thirteen and went off to Buenos Aires, with new shoes but still wearing the same scarf he'd worn in school, I said to his uncle Felipe of Anteiro:

"I bet Pedro will get rich with the grasshoppers in the theater houses."

"There aren't any grasshoppers there in the fields," said Mr Felipe, speaking to me in Spanish and overlooking my ignorance of it. "In the Pampa the only hoppers are the golden locust and the guaraneja frog and you can't train them."

And he looked at my uncle Serxio, who wasn't there, as if he would back him up.

I don't know what became of Pedro Corto. When I see grasshoppers on the hill around Midsummer's Eve, I always think of him.

Perrín's Speeches

Perrín of Buriz was a good friend of mine, may he rest in peace. He was a hunter and fisherman and knew about medicinal herbs. He was always smiling and cordial and very willing to do favors for people. He loved to take walks. He knew the sierras well, like Corda and Cadramón. In 1934 he broke a leg and had to spend a month in bed. That was when he started to dream that he was talking with animals, especially his dog Columbus. They had long conversations in which the animals told him their secrets, their life stories, their problems. Perrín would dream that he left the house and went up the hill, where he encountered a hare that was trying to get out of bed and flee. Perrín would shout to it in the secret hare language and the hare would stop and come toward him, moving its tail. They would talk. Sometimes Perrín felt like grabbing the hare, killing it and eating it in parsley sauce, but he never did. That would have been unfair. In his dreams he'd say to the hare:

"Get out of here or I'll turn into a hunter!"

And the hare would run away. But Perrín wouldn't shoot at it. He decided that, with these friendships he was making during conversations in the woods, he was going to have to stop being a hunter. He'd devote himself to fishing only. But one day he dreamed about a trout. It was a widow.

"Come on, Perrín, a widowed trout!"

"Yes, sir! A trout widow, very proper. Some young men from Luarca caught her husband. May he rest in peace, as they say!"

When Perrín awoke, he forgot the animals' language. He became flustered and asked me if there was some way to remember the foreign languages he knew when he was asleep after he woke up. I told him I'd never read anything about that, but for a start he shouldn't try to remember the whole magical language at once, just one or two words, and should do the same thing every day until he had two dozen of them. But it was very hard for him. He'd feel that he knew two or three words really well and would wake up, and nothing. One day he awoke knowing three:

"*Ta pura mikala...* And now what do I do?"

"Let's see if you remember another three tomorrow!"

He never remembered another word after that and luckily I didn't forget that "*ta pura mikala.*" I'd use it with dogs, chickens, pigeons, rabbits in the shed, and nothing, they never even noticed I was talking to them. But perhaps if Perrín of Buriz said it, something would happen.

"Say it to Columbus!"

And he did. Perrín himself told me. The dog looked at him with surprise.

"*Ta pura mikala!*"

He said it three times. The dog, saddened, left with its tail between its legs. It went off along the road to Moncín.

"*Ta pura mikala!*" Perrín shouted after him as he watched the dog leave, seeing he was losing that good hunting dog, his friend, his dear companion.

The dog left and Perrín never saw it again. Columbus the dog looked at his master first with surprise, then in fear.

"It looked like he was going to cry!"

Two years went by and Perrín went to Nouceda to hunt. He'd stopped dreaming that he could talk with animals and once in a while he'd think about his dog Columbus. If only he was there that morning! And what do you know, Columbus appears on a path next to some *xesta* plants. He lifted his head up and looked at the man who'd been his master.

"Columbus! Columbus, my boy!"

"*Ta pura mikala! Ta pura mikala!*"

The dog pronounced it very well. Perrín was scared. The dog said the famous phrase a third time.

"*Ta pura mikala!*"

He said it with a Spanish accent. Perrín – and he still wasn't over the fear when he told me about it – had to leave the woods and go back to the road by Gontán. Some invisible force pushed him out of the woods. The dog looked at him like he was in charge. And Perrín, "sad as a dog," as he said, withdrew and returned to his house, obeying the secret command. And he never went back to the woods.

"I can't! Columbus won't let me!"

Monteiro of Rubias

His name was Antón. Rubias is an area of high hills and remote pastures beside the Sor, with tall grass and thorny *xesta* bushes, meadows with bluegrass and clover, a lone birch or two, a few walnut trees in the flat parts and meadows on the lower slopes, where they cut dry grass after Midsummer. The houses of Rubias are in a high area, where there used to be a *castro*, an Iberian village, catalogued by Don Federico Menciñeira. The Andrades had a tower around there. The river, singing and frothy, flows down below amid the crags. The residents of Rubias make a living by keeping livestock in the forest. Well, they used to make a living, because with the big reforestation effort they ended up with no fields or meadows and the pine trees grow almost up to their front doors. They're all going to have to leave. Of the Monteiros, who were once nobility and are related to the Verdes of Sistallo, the only one left is Vitorino, who joined the seminarians in Mondoñedo, the ones who wear loose robes and a red sash, but lives in Barcelona now, is employed by Seat and married to a dark lass from Albacete, half gypsy. Going back through the Monteiros' family tree, you get to Fernán Pérez de Andrade the Good. Once, when they announced the visit of the late Duke of Alba to Galicia, I told Monteiro of Rubias, when I ran into him in Lugo, he should go to greet him and call him "cousin."

"Go on, we don't have that sort of relationship!" Antón replied.

He probably meant they didn't know each other very well, although he may have meant to say what the first-born son of Rubias said, which wouldn't have displeased Maurice

Barrès, who studied the theme of the *deracinés* or uprooted.

Monteiro once went to the baths by the beach at Covas. I'm talking about the elder one, Antón, not the younger one, Vitorino. He had a doctor's prescription (that is to say a prescription from the medicine man Pita of San Cobade, who's still alive and very hygienic and likes prescribing dairy products), but was supposed to take the baths during the old moon and they made him ill. He lost weight, went half deaf, got sties and, worst of all, there was a sort of shadow around him. The shadow came out of the sea with him one day and Monteiro figured it belonged to someone who'd drowned. The shadow accompanied him to Rubias and was always by his side and when winter came, it would get in bed with Monteiro, shivering.

"The shadow was a very small one," Vitorino insisted to me, having heard his father tell the story.

Yes, Antón believed the shadow was a lot smaller than him and thin because, when Antón opened a door a little and had difficulty passing through, the shadow had no problem at all. The shadow didn't eat anything. Once Monteiro put out a plate of milk and honey for it, but the shadow didn't lick a drop. Monteiro was ailing and tired and the only company he had was that shadow. He'd go out for a walk and lean on its head as if it were a cane. One day the shadow whistled a happy tune. Monteiro got a bit better and now that summer had come, Pita sent him to Covas again during the first quarter-moon.

"Let's see if you recover!" said the medicine man.

Monteiro went into the waves and the shadow went with him. When he came out, the shadow remained in the ocean. Monteiro shouted to it and spent a whole day on the beach, crying. The shadow never returned and Monteiro went back to Rubias alone. He died shortly afterward, bored, with no appetite and tired, very tired. He'd grown a beard. Once in a while he'd leap out of bed, where he spent most of the time, grab his rifle and fire a few shots out the window into the air. He got the idea that a band from Romariz should learn the song the shadow had whistled to him. But he couldn't recall it very well. He was willing to pay four thousand pesetas to the person who could do it. A short while ago, in Barcelona, Vitorino Aguiar Maseda came to see me in the hotel where I was staying. The woman from Albacete was with him. I asked Vitorino if that shadow of his father's had really existed.

"It wasn't exactly a shadow!"

And, turning to the woman from Albacete, he explained to her in Spanish:

"It was like they'd taken off his outer body and his inner body had been set free."

The woman from Albacete agreed, nodding her head.

"Oh, oh!" she said and started to cry.

"She's afraid," Vitorino explained, "the same thing could happen to our little Antonciño."

Souto of Lires' Soul

I met Souto of Lires in about 1930, more or less. He must have been around twenty years old. His name was Manuel Berdía González. His father was the owner of the mill at Lires. Little Manuel was born with a head that was a bit misshapen, his right arm was shorter than the left and his left foot was half turned around. He didn't care much about his defective head. About that time he bought a gray hat in Mondoñedo and, after a day of working at it, managed to put it on straight, that is in a vertical line with his body, even though his head was turned to the right. His short arm didn't bother him much either. He figured that for digging, shooting a rifle and playing the guitar it was even an advantage. He wanted me to write something in the weekly newspaper in Mondoñedo, *Vallibria*, about what he'd told me in the barbershop regarding the advantages of having one arm shorter than the other. And I could add something about Wilhelm II's short arm. On the other hand, what really bothered him was his foot.

"I don't deserve this, dammit!" he said to me one day.

When it was time to go for his military service, he hoped somehow they'd consider him apt for the infantry or artillery.

"On a horse, nobody notices the foot and I can still stand beside a cannon."

They classified him as completely incapacitated. A girl from Sandiás refused to have him, even though the Soutos of Lires were known as large landholders. That's when Manuel started going downhill, turning lazy, walking by himself in the woods, spending weeks in bed. His twisted foot was a problem of a cosmic, physical and moral nature. When the Creator kicked Adam and Eve out of Paradise, he told them they'd earn their bread with the sweat of their brows, but he never said, "And there shall be lame people among you." And if he didn't say it, but thought it? What a problem! Analyzing the matter, Souto of Lires became a full-blown atheist. Around then he started feeling a pounding in his chest that wouldn't let him sleep. The doctors couldn't figure out the problem. Manuel Berdía, better known as Souto of Lires, was dying. They called the Seixo priest, who had long conversations with him. It seems that for the most part there are no physical differences in the other world, there are no cripples and if there are, you don't notice them. I think the Seixo priest, in order to get around this, even cited Genesis, where it says how all the bodies of the blessed, on reaching Paradise, have a spherical shape and, since Pythagoras and Plato, the sphere is the most perfect shape of all. Souto confessed and took communion. He was quite warm and lay silent in his bed and every once in a while he'd say not even if he had twenty pesos in his jacket, when he died, would he be able to find a photographer in the other world to send two portraits, one for the Seixo priest and another for the girl from Sandiás. And one day like any other, late afternoon – it was autumn and dry leaves were blowing along the path that leads down from the Lires mill – Manuel died.

Two or three years went by. It was around St Martin and the priest from Seixo went to see the patron saint at Teixeiro. From a turnip patch by the side of the path he saw a crow land two yards away. Don Perfecto Illade Morante stared at the crow, which reminded him of somebody. Yes, sir, it was Manuel Berdía, Souto of Lires. Its head was crooked, one wing shorter than the other and its left foot twisted.

"What are you doing around here, fellow?" the priest asked.

"When you fly, you don't limp!" screamed the crow.

And off it went, up over the turnip patches to the Mestas oak grove. They talked a lot about it around the region. Don Perfecto Illade told everybody:

"In the first place, my brethren, the ways of the Lord cannot be foreseen. In the second place, hard work pays off."

Cerdeira of Marco

Xosé Onega Viador, known as Cerdeira of Marco, spent his entire life wanting to have a talking parrot. Cerdeira was a little man, sickly, always cold, who wore a black hat with a broad brim pulled down over his head. He married one of the heiresses of Sirmunde, Miz Euxenia, who was tall, buxom and fair. When Miz Euxenia died and Cerdeira found he was the owner of a fortune, he decided it was time to go buy the parrot. Besides he didn't have any children left from his marriage. In Lugo they gave him the address of a business in Barcelona that delivered parrots, cockatoos, *papagaios* and all sorts of birds. Cerdeira wrote to find out the prices. They answered, saying that in fact at that very moment they had two parrots which spoke French and would sell them to him for a good price, either the pair or separately. They sent him photographs of the parrots along with a brochure on how to care for them, their food, illnesses, etc. One of the parrots was named Briand and the other Calumet and they were from Central America. Cerdeira went to check with Domingo of Moure, agronomist and hunter, who was licensed out of León. Cerdeira was inclined to pick Briand, but Domingo of Moure preferred Calumet.

"Look how he holds his head up! He looks much more honest!"

"He looks a bit arrogant to me!" noted Cerdeira.

"That's not a bad thing in foreigners!" declared Domingo.

Cerdeira gave in and bought the parrot named Calumet. It arrived in Lugo without mishap on the Camerana bus line.

It was rather small, very restless, and had a red spot in one eye. As soon as they took it out of the box, it began to greet people.

"*Bonjour, mesdames et messieurs! Mon biscuit, s'il vous plaît!*"

"'*Biscuit*' is pound cake," said the teacher in Marco, who was from Alicante.

"Well, he's a fine one!" said Cerdeira. "Wouldn't it be sufficient to give him some wine-soaked bread with sugar on it?"

"*Voulez-vous une soupe de vin sucré?*" the man from Alicante asked him.

"*Landru au poteau!*" the parrot screamed.

The teacher explained to Cerdeira who Landru was. After that, they discussed with Domingo of Moure how to go about adapting the parrot to Galician cooking so it would stop asking for pound cake. Calumet was quiet, listening, and once in a while would scratch at its lice with its beak. That afternoon they gave it a María cookie dipped in milk and half a canned peach.

"This Calumet is turning out to be a bit expensive!" said Cerdeira.

The parrot slept on its perch, which Cerdeira had made himself, since he knew a little about carpentry and had gotten the design from the cover of a Brazilian magazine. Before turning out the light, Cerdeira told the parrot:

"I'm José Ortega, your master," in Spanish.

"*Bonsoir, papa!*" Calumet answered.

Cerdeira thought that was funny. He dreamed that he started to learn French and talked with the parrot, which went and told him about its family and what Central America and Barcelona were like. But the next morning, when Cerdeira went to take the parrot something to eat, it had flown off. Cerdeira told me himself:

"Nothing! Not a trace of it!"

For many days, morning, afternoon and night, Cerdeira searched for Calumet in the meadows, in the oak grove by Eirís, among the *xesta* bushes in Vilega, in his neighbors' houses. Nothing! Cerdeira was inconsolable at having lost him. Two years went by and he still thought about Calumet.

"It was so quick to figure out I was its owner! *Bonsoir, papa!*"

And he'd start to cry. He bought a French-Spanish dictionary in case Calumet returned. One day Cerdeira went to Lugo and sat down at Vilares to wait for the bus in the shade of some birches. He lifted his head up because almost right beside him a cuckoo was singing.

"Believe me, Don Álvaro! The cuckoo was saying 'cu-coo, cu-coo,' but in French. I can't explain it, man! The same accent Calumet had! It'd been around there! Do the books say anything about whether a parrot can marry a cuckoo?"

Cerdeira could never be consoled for the loss of Calumet, as I said. He got more and more sunken beneath his black hat. He went around with the French dictionary under his arm. He caught pneumonia and died. In the dictionary he had the photo of Calumet they'd sent him from Barcelona, with its head held high, and a sign beneath: "*On parle français.*"

Lomas of Noceda

All these Lomases I'm talking about are people who go around with weird things, miracles, spells and wonders. I was a close friend of some of them, the Lomas line with the mill in Pontigo. The son, Manuel, when he was two years old and in his crib at the mill, went sailing out the window because there was a big storm and a flood came and the road that led upward turned into a river. The crib sailed downstream and at Manuel's feet was a rat that didn't take its eyes off the baby until the crib ran aground between two willows. That adventure, which he heard his mother tell a thousand times, left Manuel with a taste for all the news there was about the Great Flood and others. When *El Progreso* of Lugo had news of some flood, Lomas read the newspaper several times, talked about the situation and argued about how much water it would take to cover Mount Carracedo:

which scares all the other mountains,
except for Montiral,
which is its equal!

The Lomas folks, because of their uncle Felipo, better known as Xaneiro, talked a lot about Weyler and some boots he had when he was commander for the last time in Cuba. Xaneiro was Weyler's assistant and in charge of shining his boots. He was chosen for his breath. A doctor named Quintana found twelve soldiers and tested their breath with a piece of glass and a bit of wax. Felipo came out on top.

"There was nobody else in the whole army whose breath was hotter than his!"

Weyler's boots had to be cleaned only with human breath and a fuzzy cloth. Weyler trained Felipo Lomas and told him:

"This leather has to last forever!"

On the advice of Dr Quintana, Xaneiro would do the cleaning at night, after supper. Each boot took him half an hour. They didn't shine, which didn't matter at all to the captain-general, but the boots were very clean and the leather was incomparably soft.

When Weyler's boots stopped making the corns he had on both feet hurt, he promoted Xaneiro to corporal. After the island was lost, Xaneiro returned to Cuba, where he married a Cantabrian with a big beauty mark on her upper lip. The woman from Santander had a quick temper, became upset over nothing and when she got jealous because Xaneiro hugged a mulatta, she turned red, so red it was scary. One day, when one of these struggles occurred, the blood rushed to her face and her beauty mark disappeared.

"It must have been a wart!" I said to him.

"It wasn't a wart! It was an Andalusian beauty mark!"

When she lost her beauty mark, the Cantabrian changed and became a hard-working, very humble woman, was no longer jealous and listened with a smile whenever her husband told stories of Weyler and his boots.

Xaneiro returned from Cuba with the Cantabrian and they lived in a beautiful house in Candedo. In the lower part were some mottled cherry trees from Santander, which have lots of flowers, spread out and bear plenty of fruit. The cherries are small and pointy, but very tasty. Next to the cherry trees is the old royal road to Miranda, with oak trees along the side as far as Recaré.

Pascuas of Lurres

Nobody knows if the joke came from his father, Mr Arximiro, or his godfather, Don Pedro Pardo, who according to him was a direct descendant of his namesake, the field marshal beheaded in the square in Mondoñedo. They named the baby Felices and since his last names were Pascuas García, he ended up as Felices Pascuas García.

"Where they teased me most was in the military."

A sergeant from Murcia, Jesualdo Fábregas, sent him around the 20th of December to visit all the other sergeants of the regiment and to the bugler as well, who was small and had a pock-marked face.

"You go there and say your name."

Pascuas of Lurres would go and introduce himself, saying:

"Felices Pascuas!"

"Thank you," they'd answer him.

"He sent me like a postcard around all Girona! And it was raining!"

Pascuas of Lurres was bothered his whole life by the joke of Felices Pascuas. Short, chubby, blondish, with sparkling eyes, what he liked best was to read the newspaper aloud and talk about the sieges of Girona, which he knew all about, except the date, and anybody listening to him would think they'd taken place in 1927, when Pascuas had to go serve the king. Girona, according to him, had been laid siege to by the French, helped by the Moors... Pascuas didn't understand why in music there was "The Siege of Zaragoza" and no sieges of Girona. Pascuas knew "The Siege of Zaragoza" by heart, but what he really understood was the record about the shooting of Ferrer and he could do the volleys really well, so well that, instead of one or two, he'd imitate eight or ten, standing up, dramatic, and letting himself fall on the last one, like Ferrer in the trench at Montjuïc. When he turned forty, he noticed that for his entire life, when he went along the Pacios road from Lurres to Lugo or to the St Luke festivities in Mondoñedo, he walked along, imitating the drum:

"Pum, pum, ratapum, pum, pum!"

Without a drum he couldn't walk. He developed a drum complex. He bought one and learned to play it. It had a really good sound and he found a march that fit his short legs well. He got to a point where he couldn't walk without the drum. He got up and hung the instrument from his belt. He'd go from the meadow to the field and went along playing the drum. He'd take the wheat to the mill and went along playing the drum. He no longer took a step without being encouraged, I could even say pushed, by the drum. It would talk to him:

"Get up, Pepiño, we're going to go dig!"

And he'd go out to the field with the drum. His family said he'd gone mad, but he was happy and made the *figa* sign to his nephews and nieces, telling them to go away. Finally he began to read the newspaper with the drum and in his final years he no longer spoke. He said everything with the drum. The last time I saw him I was going along the road to Vilares to wait for the bus and Pascuas was in the threshing area, up next to the hayloft, with the drum next to him. I called to him:

"What a life, Pascuas!"

And he answered me with a cheerful, friendly drum roll.

A few months later I heard he'd died. The priest at Ribeira told me that, when he was in Mondoñedo for spiritual exercises and wanted to confess him, Pascuas asked to do it by drum.

"Crazy fellow, totally crazy! He was so good, so good, I let him play what he wanted! May the Lord watch over him!"

Porteiro of Mouros

Mouros is on the other side of Corda. There are good fields, oak groves and a thick forest. The houses are at the bottom of the valley, next to the river, in the area they call O Chao, the Flatland. The first house, which is always nicely whitewashed, is Porteiro's mill. The river is a small branch of the Sor, happy and leaping, and further down from the mill it slows down to mirror the birches and willows. The village of Mouros is poor. The reforestation left the people there without areas to pasture livestock. All the young ones have left for Switzerland or Germany and pretty soon there won't be any Mouros left and you won't be able to see the blue smoke from the chimneys down there from Portela.

Once I asked Porteiro, to tease him, if there were Moors in Mouros. He looked at me with a serious expression on his face and took his time answering. Finally he said:

"And if there weren't, where would the name have come from?"

I tried to clarify if the Moors of Mouros were a thing of the past or there were still some left, where they could be found, if they belonged to that secret group that guards treasures, magical beings or regular people, farmers or clog-makers. And the only thing I could get out of Porteiro was that this business about the Moors of Mouros was a big mystery. Years went by and I never saw Porteiro, then a little while ago I heard he'd died and they told me a story. Porteiro was coming from Lugo and after he'd crossed the bridge, two hundred steps from his mill, he saw a Moor sitting on the branch of a chestnut tree. It was around dusk. The Moor was amusing himself throwing a gold coin to the ground, then he'd whistle and the coin would fly back into his hand again. Porteiro stood there for half an hour, astonished, watching the game. It was already completely dark, but the coin glowed in the blackness and it was easy to follow how it flew. The Moor was no longer visible. The only thing you could see was the coin falling and you could hear the whistle that made it fly back up.

"It's for you!" said a happy, childlike voice.

And there was the coin, in front of Porteiro, glowing like an ember. Porteiro took the coin, an Isabel II half-ounce. That night he got up many times from his bed to look at it again and again. It was lovely rubbing that gold in the night. Porteiro was afraid the devilish Moor would whistle and the coin would fly away back to him. And how did the coin hear the whistle? Through Isabel II's ear? Wouldn't it be a good idea to plug it up with a bit of wax? But the Moor didn't whistle. Porteiro and the Moor became fast friends. Once in a while the Moor would give the miller a coin. Until one day the Moor confessed to Porteiro he had only one coin left, with Amadeo on it, and the ones he'd given him no longer worked for the game: once he'd given them away, he could no longer play with them because by giving them away he relinquished his power over them.

"So why did you give them to me, man?"

"Because you believed there were Moors around here."

Porteiro suggested that with the coin the Moor had left – and Porteiro, although he used the familiar form of address, always called him "Mr Moor" – they could go to Lugo, Vilalba and Mondoñedo. With the Moor dressed that way he could pass for Mustapha the Magician and play the game in front of an audience, offering the coin as a prize to anybody who could catch it as it flew, while charging one peseta to play. The Moor was reluctant at first, but in the end he agreed and went with Porteiro around St Froilan to

Monterroso and the fair at Palas, then down to St Luke and the three fairs in Vilalba. Nobody even got close to grabbing the Amadeo coin. The Moor and Porteiro made around four thousand pesetas. They traveled at night, reaching the fairs at daybreak. The Moor would eat octopus and beef stew. He also liked noodle soup.

"So what'll we do with the money?" Porteiro asked the Moor.

"Buy me some good clogs and some glasses for short-sightedness. There's nothing worse for the eyes than watching gold fly around!"

Porteiro bought him the clogs and eyeglasses. The Moor went on living in that chestnut tree, but never told Porteiro how he got in and out, nor what he did there. He told him stories about the Arabs. When Porteiro fell ill, the Moor went to see him twice and sat at the foot of his bed. That's what Porteiro said anyway, because nobody in the house ever saw Mustapha the Magician come in. Porteiro died and underneath his pillow, in an empty cigar-box, were eleven gold coins, all of them with a little bit of wax on them, in Isabel II or Carlos III's ear. Sure they were friends, but just in case. Porteiro's children poked at the chestnut tree where the Moor lived, but never found the treasure they thought they would. It was said the Moor would come out to play with his coin in another chestnut tree, beside the river, and throw the coin into the water. The people of Mouros would hide there at night, but nobody ever managed to spot the Moor. Porteiro's children still have the coins and will show them to anyone who wants to see them.

Areeiro of Pordade

The people of Pordade built their houses along the river. The first one, almost at the foot of the forest of Rende, is Puga Vello's. I think a grandson of Mr Marcelino, who was the owner when I passed that way in the summer, lives there now. Mr Marcelino wore sideburns like Alfonso XII's and when he went to Lugo to offer himself to Pepe Benito, which was always around St Froilan, he would come back with a hundred newspapers under his arm, a gift from his boss, which afterward, when he got home, he'd put in chronological order. Every night he'd read something. In 1940, shortly before he died, he was still reading *El Debate* papers from 1931. The last house, which is in the low, fertile area, belongs to the Areeiros. At the tall grain bin, you go from the house over a bridge of seven stone slabs, which in autumn is full of large, yellow pumpkins sitting in the sun. The river has a different name in each section. It's called, in order, Monte Stream, Cruz Stream, Old Forge River, Vilar River and finally Pagos. It's called Vilar River in Pordade. The monks at Meira had a forge and mill around there. The Areeiros are of Germanic stock, blond, tall, with blue eyes. I was a close friend of Manuel, who was a gelder and bagpipe player. For his work – as he called his veterinary art – he used a German sublimate that he'd buy in my father's pharmacy and the black paper the tube was wrapped in had a skull and crossbones.

"You see?" he'd say to me, showing me the tube. "Very, very deadly! To be safe you have to handle it with tweezers. Your father really trusts me!"

The reeds of his bagpipe were Italian, Venturini brand,

Alessandria della Paglia, via Bargello, 17. I remember it as well as if I were seeing it now, that little wooden box the reeds came in with its green label, the Savoy coat of arms and the tiny letters that stated the Venturini brothers were providers for the "Reggia Armata." They sent them C.O.D. from Barcelona.

Manuel had a cousin named Secundino, who was born with one leg shorter than the other. Among people from Lugo there is a high probability that a lame man will become a tailor. Secundino became a tailor and went to Buenos Aires. He did well there and one day, remembering his cousin Manuel, sent him some bagpipe reeds with a fellow from Bretoña. They were Bulgarian. They came in a box of gold-colored tin. And on the cover was a bagpipe. In red letters it said: "*Toute la musique. I. Muroff, de la Royale Societé Folklorique. Sophie. Bulgarie.*"

"Bulgaria! Look how far the bagpipe's traveled!" Manuel of Areeiro said to me.

I didn't know there were bagpipes in Bulgaria. The years go by and I'd forgotten I knew that thanks to Manuel's bagpipe reeds when the other day I read in a French newspaper about Boris of Bulgaria and it said the Bulgarian had been poisoned after returning from a meeting with Hitler. The article ended by saying so long as the Bulgarian bagpipe sings, the good Tsar will be remembered. The Bulgarian bagpipe with Muroff reeds like the ones on my friend Manuel of Areeiro's bagpipe, which he played in the church courtyard at Seixo, next to the tall yew tree, at dusk on the feast of Our Lady of August!

Braulio of Regadas

Regadas has a very fitting name because five or six streams or *regueiros* that start up high, called As Pías, come to rest down below in the valley and merge in the Couzo River, then go on to the Mandeo. Birches, poplars, willows, alders, grow around there and in Reimonde there are some wicker bushes, which are lovely to look at when winter comes and on the end of the yellow wicker branches there are still a few silvery leaves. The woodcocks take flight and the full marshes of January shine when the pale rays of the sun hit them. The Ligueiras' house is up a little from the church and that's the part that's actually called Regadas. Heading down to Couzo are Saabeira, Froxán, Xobe, Millarenta and Camiña, rye fields on the slope and meadows below. When he had some free time, Braulio of Ligueira or Braulio of Regadas would go otter hunting. He'd tan the hides, eat the loin in a good sauce and melt the animal's fat down to make a cream for rheumatism. Braulio would go to my father's pharmacy to buy tincture of iodine, always with that big pipe in his mouth. Braulio had miraculously survived being hit by lightning. A storm caught him by surprise in the early afternoon during the hay-mowing month by the ford at Couzo and to get to Sanxeés more quickly he took the short cut, where the branches of chestnuts were showing off their flowers. There was continuous lightning and thunder rolled again and again. It was raining hard. Braulio stopped beneath a chestnut tree and at that moment they grabbed him by the arm.

"A tall man," he explained. "Well, a round, golden man…"

One of that man's hands grabbed him hard, lifted him into the air and threw him down the hill from the woods. Braulio must have flown because he fell a hundred meters away in a marshy area. And while Braulio was heading toward the mud, a spark hit the chestnut tree and split it in three parts. The chestnut was smoking. Braulio was saved thanks to the unknown, round, golden man. He wouldn't listen to explanations they gave him about the wind caused by lightning and they told him the round, golden fellow must have been the light from the flash. Against all other opinions, Braulio had an argument: the arm the stranger had grabbed and pulled so hard had grown by four inches.

"I can bring a certificate from a tailor in Lugo saying that before the lightning my arms were the same length."

He stretched both arms out in front of me and I looked at them, touched them and measured them with a measuring-tape, surprised and impressed.

"And who could have grabbed you? Your guardian angel?" I asked him.

"Or a friendly ghost, or a dead soul that was going by, or St Cosmas..."

Belle of Seixo

I have mentioned Seixo, the Romanesque arches of its façade with their capitals showing round-faced monks holding long-necked doves in their hands. On the sunny side is a large chestnut grove reaching as far as the river and along the fertile valley are green meadows extending as far as the few houses, all white and covered with blue slate from Murás. They grow corn on both sides of the river. The Belles' house is the first one when you cross the ford at Rillada. I was good friends with the oldest son, Nicolás Picos González, who died of tetanus. He was tall and dark, like all the Belles, and a hunter. He bragged about having shot a bear in Asturias and how nobody there had killed more wolves than he had. And among the wolves was one called Quinto. I never found out who gave it that name.

It wasn't easy to get Quinto. Nicolás Belle discovered when it was out wandering around, it always ended up at daylight in the Miral forest, entering through the underbrush of *xesta* bushes, small oaks, broom and strawberry trees along the short cut by the spring, which flows right where a tax collector called Liñares turned up dead. According to Euxenio Basanta, Vilalba's medical examiner, they stuffed the tax receipts he was carrying in his briefcase down his throat with a stick. Well, that's where the wolf named Quinto entered after stopping to drink in the stream, since according to Nicolás it knew it wouldn't find water until it came out on the other side of the forest. Nicolás Belle visited the priest in Seixo, borrowed a stole from him and went and put it right at the point where the wolf entered the forest. Belle climbed up an old oak tree to wait, not without rubbing garlic on the soles of his shoes so he wouldn't smell like a human. At dawn Quinto arrived. When he saw the stole, he stopped and after thinking about it circled around, looking for another way into the forest. Belle fired and killed it. It was an old, gray-haired wolf with a big scar on its neck.

Many went to see Quinto's scar because it had a history. Quinto fought once with the sexton of Sismondi. The sexton was coming back from a one-year anniversary mass and the wolf appeared on the bridge. The sexton spat three times and started to whistle. The wolf sat down and opened its mouth. The sexton took off his jacket, but the wolf didn't move. The sexton's name was Lourido. Well, Lourido broke into a cold sweat. He moved closer to the little wooden railing of the bridge and started looking at the water in the river. Without realizing what he was doing, he began getting undressed and throwing his clothes into the river. He also threw in his hat and the bag where he had his robe and rochet. As naked as the day he was born, he went up to the wolf and, turning his face aside so the beast couldn't sink its sharp teeth in him, sunk his own in the wolf's neck and pulled hard. The wolf whined, broke loose and ran off. Lourido's mouth was full of blood and hairs from the wolf. Naked, stumbling, he reached his house. When she saw him, his wife fell in a faint to the ground. A little while later Lourido got red spots on his face, his teeth fell out and his stomach became inflamed. A green spittle drooled out of his lips. It was all the effect of the wolf's blood according to the knowledgeable ones of the region, among them Borrallo of Lagoa. And in a few weeks Lourido was gone.

In India they tell about some royal castes where the children born in the palace while their fathers were far away, fighting wars, showed they were legitimate even if the maharaja hadn't slept with the maharani for two or three years by drinking the blood of a wolf without anything happening to them. If they were the children of adultery, they would die after seven days. Obviously Lourido was not the legitimate son of a maharaja from India. But he was much respected – may he rest in peace, reciting the liturgy in style.

Couto of Carracedo

Yesterday I was talking with a fellow who sold cookies around the province of Lugo (so he told me), waved to me friendly-like and invited me to a drink when I ran into him in Elixio's tavern

"I met a friend of yours over in Murias. A guy named Couto, who said he'd built a flying machine with a model you designed."

And it was true, except the model wasn't mine. I'd met Couto of Carracedo at some relatives' when he went there in the fall to fix the mattresses. He was small and weakly and his voice sounded like it came from the grave. He helped with threshing chestnuts and always organized a chestnut festival or *magosto* for the kids. I had an issue of the magazine *Minotaur*, which had the designs for Leonardo's flying machines built by a French engineer named Fournier. I remember his last name because of Don Heraclio, the card guy. The Frenchman had managed to build one of Leonardo's machines. Couto of Carracedo told me he might be able to build one.

"I might just fly over Mondoñedo!" he told me.

I never saw Couto of Carracedo again and don't know if he figured out how to build Leonardo da Vinci's flying machines or not. What Couto wanted was to fly over the ocean. Couto had done his military service in Valencia, where he married a widow who made pants for priests. The relationship went well. The widow served him tomato sandwiches and, to drink, *horchata*. On Sundays there was paella at the house of the Valencian woman's mother, who also liked the look of Couto and snuggled up to the soldier a little too close when they looked out the window to see if her daughter was coming with dessert.

"I looked out of the corner of my eye at my future mother-in-law, smiled at her and gave her a few discrete pats on the backside."

One day the widow suddenly hugged him.

"Oh, Rosendito, you're the spitting image of a boyfriend I had who died from tuberculosis!"

Afterward Couto felt a bit apprehensive because he had very clean habits. Thank heaven his battalion was sent to the Pyrenees. Up there the air was healthy and Couto earned a bit of extra money helping to shear sheep in the town of Huesca. He became friends with a lame smuggler and gave him some of his bread every day and grub when it was lentils and ham. The smuggler gave Couto a suitcase with a false bottom and a good spy-glass, a spy-glass of yellow metal – I had it in my very hands – and a plaque that said it was property of ship lieutenant Lavièbre. I made this Lavièbre fellow into an admiral and wrote a few stories about him set in the taverns in Brittany, France. Years later I heard that the wet-nurse of General Weygand – whose mysterious origin is associated with a royal family of Europe – was Lavièbre by birth and the Lavièbres were Saint-Malo pirates, buddies of Cratcoördam and Bruc the Red.

It was good to know Couto was alive and still remembered me. If I had a week's vacation right now, I'd go to Muras, to Xohán Blanco's tavern, and I bet I'd find Couto telling the story of the Valencian widow and her friendly mother, the flying machines, how healthy the air is in the Pyrenees, how we first ate snails and how he got a case of hiccups that lasted a month because the sauce was so spicy. From that time on he loved to sip hot, sugared wine.

Barcas and the Fox

Barcas of Moura is a clog-maker from Loboso who travels around the better part of Pastoriza and Terra Chá in the fall, doing clog-work: he makes soles as well as wooden shoes, soles for clogs or the gay, light, little slippers with their tops prettily cut away, which are undoubtedly the loveliest female footwear in the world. While plying his trade in Vilares do Santo, Barcas sat on a stump to roll a cigarette and, looking at a pile of wood shavings, noticed it moving as if somebody were inside, breathing, sleeping soundly and peacefully. The pile wasn't that big and Barcas thought it was probably a dog, one of those yellow mutts that yap at people along the roads in Galicia. He kicked at the wood shavings, scattering the pile, until he discovered what was hiding there. It was a fox. Barcas closed the shed door and then poked the sleeping fellow with a branch to rouse it. The fox opened its right eye, yawned twice and finally smiled.

"That's right, it smiled at me!"

It was a very small fox with fine fur and a tail almost as long as its body.

"You're so small!" Barcas said.

"That's because I'm a dwarf, Barcas! I was born premature, at three months!"

The fox spoke Galician quite well, with the accent they have around there, where they say "awther" instead of "other" and "thrashing floor" for "threshing floor." Barcas likes to talk and enjoyed the conversation with the fox, which must have been the first conversation ever between a fellow from Loboso and the long-tailed one.

During their conversation the fox said its name was Anisette.

"Anisette?" I asked Barcas.

"That's right, Anisette! It said it very clearly, six or seven times!"

So this Anisette goes and asks Barcas if he wouldn't mind making it some high-topped clogs with pointed toes.

"Foxes don't wear clogs!" Barcas told Anisette.

"Obviously you've never been to Monfero!"

In Monfero, according to Anisette, is an old fox who has rheumatism, is very wise and wears clogs with linings in them.

"Lately it had pieces of tire put on them for soles so they wouldn't make any noise. It likes to hang around Curtis, watching the train go by."

Barcas made four clogs for Anisette and the fox tried them on in the shed and paraded around, despite twisting its feet once in a while, the back legs in particular. Anisette even asked him to wrap the clogs up in paper and tie the parcel because it was going to put them away until they were needed. Barcas wrapped them up and when he was done with his clog-work in Vilares, headed back to Loboso. Anisette the dwarf-fox went along with him a ways. When the two friends said goodbye on the hill in Ventos, Anisette asked Barcas a question:

"I almost forgot! Who's the leader of France?"

"A guy named De Gaulle. Why do you want to know?"

"Well, there's a fox over in Meira and when several of us go hunting, it always catches the biggest chicken, stands over it and shouts, 'Who's the leader of France?'"

Barcas never saw Anisette the dwarf-fox, born prematurely, again. He tells me this sadly while we're drinking a cup of red wine in a tavern in Mondoñedo.

Manuel Regueira

I had just finished giving a lecture in the Galician Center in Madrid and was talking with some ladies when somebody slapped me on the back. I turned around and saw Manuel Regueira López. I had been friends with his brother Celso, who was a watch repairman of sorts and every September would set traps for the badgers. He ate tough meat, well done, with tasty gravy and made shaving brushes for his friends. He lived near Xidulfe, in the highest, wildest part of Terra de Miranda, where it looks out over the Eo River with its clear waters and the weary, blue peaks of Asturias can be seen off in the distance. Celso was short and fat and, like the King of Scotland in Villon, half his face was red:

Where is the King of Scotland,
the one they say half his face was red,
crimson as an amethyst,
from his chin up to his forehead?

One day five or six years ago, a fellow from Xidulfe, seeing me on Reina Street in Lugo, told me Celso had died.

"He had a stroke and for seven days was unable to move his foot or hand or speak. On the eighth day he opened one eye, looked at the children gathered around him, crying, and said, 'Get the mice away from the cheese, you lazy things!'"

With that, he died. The day he was buried the family went up to the attic to get a couple of cheeses that were hanging there to age in a wire basket because they were planning to give them to the pallbearers, but all the cheeses had been nibbled at by mice, despite the metal shield and birch lid. How had the dying man known the mice were after the cheese? From what point and with what vision had he been observing this world? A dark mystery I cannot explain.

When Manuel Regueira finished his military service, for which he was stationed in the capital, he remained there, working in a bakery, from where he went to work with a chiropodist who had his practice on Toledo Street. Manuel had always been fond of sculpture and in the bakery made rolls in the shape of people, horses and birds for New Year and other holidays. When he became the chiropodist's assistant, he would make molds of the feet of regular customers, before and after his boss had worked on their corns, and if it so happened that the customer was famous and they were talking about him in the newspapers, he'd put the plaster cast in the shop window, with corns and without them. When the Infanta Isabel died, despite the fact it was during the Republic, La Chata's feet went on display. One day, as I was passing the master chiropodist's shop, there were two right feet on display, one full of corns of all shapes and sizes, in the strangest places, and the other nice and clean. A sign said: "Right foot of the Most Excellent Señor Don Félix de Llanos y Torriglia, Elected Member of the Royal Academy of History, before and after being treated in this establishment." And next to the two feet, dedicated to the chiropodist, was one of Llanos y Torriglia's works, *Felipe II's Daughters* or something.

Manuel managed to save up a little and married off a daughter to the heir of a dairy with stables on a street in the Salamanca neighborhood, near a bath-house. He's fat, smokes blond tobacco and spends his time cleaning off the cows, swatting flies and turning on the fan in the basement where his son-in-law's cows feed. If only he could take them to the cool pastures in Xidulfe!

Sabelo of Bouzamo

I could tell you a lot about Sabelo of Bouzamo, but for now all I'm only going to tell you is that he taught a fox to whistle. When his parish priest went down to Mondoñedo for spiritual exercises, Sabelo accompanied him, taking his trained fox along. They gave the priest a room with a balcony overlooking Negrillos Street, called that because of the trees, and Sabelo sat down beside them until nightfall. When he figured his pastor had had his supper in the room, he and the fox whistled a duet. People gathered around, women on their way to Mr Daniel's baking oven with *empanadas*, it being the eve of St Christopher, and some priests came out onto their balconies. There was a lot of applause.

Sabelo would go hunting for otter in the Miño River and as well as the fur he sold the fat from along the animal's back to people with rheumatism. He'd done his military service in Salamanca, where he had a sweetheart called María Starch because she did fancy ironing jobs and ruffles on bullfighters' shirts and priests' rochets. She could make anything look shiny and ruffled. Sabelo went back to Bouzamo with the intention of returning to Salamanca to marry María, but she wrote to him, saying that a lawyer from around there, one rainy morning when she was making a delivery, accidentally ran into her with his umbrella and as a result María had lost her left eye.

"Don Álvaro, I still would have married María, but in *The Secretary of Lovers* I didn't find the letter you had to write in case your girlfriend lost an eye when you weren't there."

Sabelo told me how he'd sucked so hard on a red pencil, staring at a blank sheet of paper, trying to draft an answer to

María, he'd had stomach problems for a year. He remained a bachelor his whole life, hunting, strolling lazily along the paths of Terra de Miranda. On any path, at any time of year, Sabelo could be seen whistling, followed by Nero, his watchdog. He always had a bundle with a good ration of ham and a full wineskin and would greet his friends in French.

"*Bonjour!*" he'd say even if it were evening.

Sometimes he couldn't sleep and then he'd walk to Foz, where the lapping of the waves would cure him.

"And what became of the whistling fox?" I asked him one day.

"The world's full of contradictions! If I told you the chickens ate him, you wouldn't believe me!"

He put his closed fist up to his mouth, kissed his thumb and I couldn't get another word out of him.

Ruzos of Beiral

I never met Ruzos of Beiral, but I was good friends with a nephew of his named Evaristo, who lived in Oubelle, at the end of the lake, where there's a green marsh which, when it fills up with winter rains, reaches halfway up the birch trees, covers the road to Noste and floods the lands that were previously flax fields and are now meadows and cornfields. The road to Noste passes by the Focay dolmen, where there's a fat Moor, dressed in red, keeping watch over a treasure. Pedro Nistal, the Maragato from Empalme, who had three marriageable daughters, told me how the Moor once came out to the road, when he still used to carry wine in skins, and asked him to fill a pitcher for him, which was made of gold. The Moor drank up the wine right away, burped and praised the beverage without complaining about the leathery taste that so bothered Farruquiño Montenegro when he guzzled Castilian wine, according to Valle-Inclán. He then went back to his hiding place without paying, which made the Nistal fellow hopping mad. Years later, when Nistal had gotten old, the neighbors used to see him near the dolmen, shaking his cane in the air, insulting the Moor and yelling at him to pay the peseta he owed for the pitcher of wine.

Ruzos was an expert angler and as soon as the season opened, he'd drop all his work and take off with his fishing poles to the local rivers. He made a living from the trout he sold to the inns and taverns and went as far as the kingdom of León to do it.

"Did he go to Asturias too?" I asked.

"No, because he didn't care much for the Asturians. He thought they were loud mouths."

Ruzos of Beiral was a great one with a fishing pole, but wanted people to think he had his own special secrets, strange liquors he'd put the worms in for the purpose of softening them up and so they'd lure the trout with their scent. He said he'd bought them from some Hungarians at a St Froilan fair and in addition the Hungarians had shown him how to cook snails. The first time I heard you could eat snails was from the priest at Oubelle. He told an uncle of mine:

"That friend of yours, Ruzos, eats snails. He ought to be going to confession for that, dammit, it's just the same as if he'd broken the sixth commandment!"

My uncle Xusto, who was also a priest and had been in Madrid and gone to the Apollo to see the cabaret performers and to bullfights, defended the spicy snail sauce. The abbot of Oubelle said something back that I can't repeat here.

When he was with his close friends, Ruzos used to tell them how he'd come to understand the trout's life inside out, its work and time off, love affairs and bad habits. He insisted one day he'd be able to fish using words, that is speaking trout language.

"Because I know how to tell them what's best for them!"

His nephew Evaristo once assured me he saw him catch a trout in the pool at Baño while whistling. Ruzos stood on the bank to whistle, near some birches. Once in a while he'd stop, eat a grasshopper and toss one to the trout. The trout kept moving closer, so close there was barely enough water to cover it. Ruzos threw more grasshoppers. The trout ate. Ruzos would whistle and the trout would answer. And then, using a forked oak branch he had with three prongs and really sharp points, Ruzos skewered the trout and threw it onto land.

"The trout was crying," Evaristo says to me, "but my uncle kept hitting it on the head and yelling, 'Oh you stupid, stupid donkey of a fish!'"

Fishing was Ruzos' downfall. Once he said that to study trout science better he was going to sleep in the river, which is what he did. The following day he was all battered and a month later he died. His nephew shook his head and repeated this adage:

They say the man who fishes with a rod
loses more than he makes.

Bertoldo of Reades

If I go to the capon festival in Vilalba again this year, I'm sure I'll run into Bertoldo of Reades and we'll talk for a while. He always shows up in the town square, a scarf wrapped around his neck, looking down his nose at people, bargaining to beat the band and in the end he always gets two good birds, a gift for a lawyer from Madrid. The only thing I know about the lawyer is his name's Mr Martín. Every year Bertoldo limps better and better. His limp was the topic of many conversations in the parishes of the old estates of Miragaia and Grandela. Bertoldo was going from Cospeito to his house on a fall evening, when it was raining hard, some thirty years ago. He was young then, tall and strong, and wore a small beret on his head so his curly hair would show. His eyes were clear and sparkling and he had a hooked nose and fair skin. When he traveled, even if he didn't go by bicycle, but caught the bus to Lugo in Martiñán, he wore his pants clipped to his ankles with metal fasteners. He had two or three sweethearts and when winter was over, he'd go around buying and selling sheep. Like I said, this Bertoldo was on his way home, getting soaked because that day it was raining buckets and the wind was blowing hard. At a curve in the road he ran into three strange fellows sharing a single umbrella. All three were lame, one in the right leg, the other in the left and the fellow in the middle, the shortest of the three, almost a midget, in both legs.

"Good afternoon!" Bertoldo greeted them.

"You don't have to get wet, you know. It's only because you want to!" said the one with the lame right leg.

"The umbrella is too small for all of us!" responded Bertoldo.

"It stretches as much as it needs to!" insisted the one with the lame left leg.

Bertoldo didn't accept the invitation and kept on walking. He kept going until he heard a whistle that felt like a needle in his ears. He turned around and it was the small fellow with the double limp whistling. Without knowing how, Bertoldo, who was intrigued by that whistle, found himself in the midst of the group of crippled fellows, under the umbrella, which had grown when he joined the group and now had the air of a large, black cloud. Several crows were perched on the ribs of the umbrella and everybody knows how the rain makes them cranky. When the four under the umbrella reached the crossroads at Mostende, the fellow with two lame legs, who was holding the umbrella, closed it.

"That's all for *le parapluie!*" he said.

And the three cripples flew off with the crows toward the branches of a nearby chestnut and disappeared. Some burs fell on Bertoldo, who wondered if he was drunk.

"*Le parapluie!*"

Bertoldo had never heard that word, which proves his story is true. When he saw the crows disappear toward the chestnut, Bertoldo continued on alone. He'd gone about a hundred steps when he realized he was limping. It was his left leg. His knee kept bending outward and his foot made a kind of arc in the air. One of the times his foot flew out, his cycling clip came loose and ended up in the ditch. Bertoldo began to cry and since then has walked with a limp.

This story, I repeat, was told all around. In the wintertime, in somebody's kitchen, or a Saturday at the barbershop, they still talk about him. And nobody can figure out why it happened.

Secundino Prieto

I had a friend, Secundino Prieto, who'd been sick for several years and they couldn't find the cause of his illness. Secundino was an intelligent and very lucid analyzer of his sickness. He'd sit by the door of his house, next to the fig tree, contemplating the little valley and nearby mountains, and philosophize.

"But does something hurt?" I'd ask.

"No, nothing hurts, you know! I'm just sick. Isn't that enough?"

Secundino, who was pale, tired, with no appetite, except for a few sudden cravings, the ones least able to be satisfied, like asking in January, with snow on the ground, to be brought ripe cherries from the tree by the threshing floor, confessed to me once he'd managed to look inside his body and seen how it worked.

"Just like a clock! There must be a part that doesn't work, that's come loose, but since I'm not a doctor, I cannot tell where the problem is!"

Secundino remembered when he'd noticed the first symptoms of his illness, but wasn't sure, blaming the tax collectors who gave him a fright when they discovered him with two sacks of sugar he'd bought in Lugo to raise some mules, which at the time were each worth more than fifteen thousand pesetas. Or it could be from a cold night when he may have caught a strong draft on his way back from spending an hour with a girl he had over in Fillade, whose name was Rosiña and who he was after to get her to lift her skirts. He noticed something had come loose inside him.

"It was as if they'd unbuttoned the door to my liver or the fly to my spleen or kidneys."

And he confessed to me that "unbutton" was the exact term because for several weeks it seemed to him he needed to spit a button out. If he'd spat it out, he probably wouldn't be sick now. One day Secundino had an idea. What if he could pass his illness onto somebody else? Not to do him any harm, because he wouldn't want to do anything to hurt another person, or to get revenge or because he had it in for anyone. No, if he passed his illness onto somebody else, he'd give it to a friend, someone he could talk to, go for a walk with to Lugo or Miragres de Saavedra with a good *empanada* or to Foz to swim at the end of August.

"While I was considering the matter, Don Álvaro," he said while spinning his beret around on his half-bald head with his right hand, "I felt a bit guilty. Guilty in a special way. If I got well and married Rosiña, what part of this business did I need to give to my friend, if indeed I needed to share anything with him?"

He told me confidentially he'd made a list of friends to whom he wouldn't mind passing along his illness, which wasn't so awful, didn't smell bad, didn't have any lesions and didn't need bandages or even medicine.

"I'm like a clock that's running slow, just running slow, nothing more."

So he'd put me on his list of friends. He asked me to forgive him for telling me about this bold plan and if it were necessary, he said, I should know that on the matter of eating and drinking I wouldn't have a problem. I'd always have pesos in my pocket, wouldn't need to work and as far as Rosiña was concerned, whatever we decided…

"You know there's money in this for you, of course!"

The worst thing was that Secundino didn't know how to pass his disease onto somebody else.

"In Herbade there's a fellow about my height, who looks kind of like me. A nice chap, from the Tella family. What do you think?"

But how to put Secundino's disease in this Herbade fellow's body? The latter was very humble and honorable, always smiling, and had dark, curly hair. Secundino got sicker every day and noticed more and more buttons coming loose inside him, especially when there was an old quarter-moon. And it must have really been true they were coming loose, even though the doctors said there was nothing wrong with him and he should go back to work. One day he got up early and ordered the bed changed, using the finest sheets. Then he lay down and died. He can't have had any buttons left *in situ*.

Herdeiro of Vintes

A few months ago I ran into Secundino Pacios, better known as Herdeiro of Vintes. He asked me if a cousin of his, Felipe Marful, alias Cachazas, had told me the story of a pitcher that he, Secundino, on his way to sell a mule in Cacabelos, had bought there. Secundino, when he talks to me, takes off the cap he wears shoved down as far as his eyebrows and sticks it under his arm. I can tell you Cachazas was more than half an hour making up his mind to tell me the story.

"You probably won't believe me!" he said.

And, knowing Cachazas liked a serious conversation and used philosophical statements and proverbs, I blurted out:

"I can handle the story, Cachazas!"

I meant that I was willing to listen to the whole story. So, Herdeiro of Vintes, at the big fall fair in Cacabelos, had bought a pitcher made of white clay. He took the pitcher home and put it in the cupboard. He didn't use it. One day he was going to take it out, but decided to use a different pitcher, a clay one from Mondoñedo, sitting next to it. Then the white clay pitcher spoke to Herdeiro in Spanish:

"Hey, put some wine in me!" it said.

Herdeiro got scared and didn't want to take it out, but his wife came in – she has the airs of those fancy people in Mesía, stubborn like them, and her nose is a bit out of joint – grabbed the pitcher and filled it with wine. They both drank in silence and since the pitcher didn't say anything, they put it back in its place.

"The pitcher," Cachazas told me, "didn't say a thing. But when it was back in its place, it started to dance. While it was dancing, it bumped against the other pitchers and pots. Made a mess on the pantry shelf. Then fell to the ground and broke…"

Cachazas' theory was the same as that of Herdeiro of Vintes: the pitcher had gotten drunk. But Cachazas had more to say. He stood up, came over to the grain bin, looked me straight in the eye and asked:

"Does that pitcher sound like some drunk you find in a play or book?"

Whenever he went to Lugo or Coruña, if there was a play, Cachazas would go to see it. When I was a boy and the Montjuïc Company came to Mondoñedo, Cachazas would roll into town and sit in the front row for *Noche de lobos*, *La malquerida* and *Canción de cuna*. I thought about it and gave him the name of the first drunk who came to mind.

"Well, yes, an Englishman, John Falstaff."

"He was fat, right?"

I promised to explain to Cachazas who Falstaff was and planned to give him a copy of *The Merry Wives of Windsor* and *Henry IV* by Shakespeare, but Cachazas left for Caracas to spend some time with a daughter there, who had married well and even had a TV in the house – six or seven sets, all over the house – and he never came back. His heart stopped while he was having a cold drink. When I went to Caracas myself, I visited his daughter at her husband's store on Sábana Grande Street.

"And didn't he say something before he died?" I asked her.

Cachazas' daughter looked at me with her blue eyes, saw I was fond of her father and sorry about his passing and she understood.

"Don't you think if he'd said anything before he died, he'd have wanted us to tell you?"

Then out of the mouth of Cachazas' daughter, who was just like her father in her gestures and slow way of speaking, came this:

"Life is but a dream and dreams are only dreams!"

Neira of Pardomonte

I never met the most famous of the Neiras of Pardomonte, Don Felipe, who was in the last Carlist War and bought a horse from the heir of a Basque priest. The priest rode around the countryside with a nephew beside him to keep watch over him while he slept and to make him chocolate. Angry, the nephew followed his uncle, who would never loan him his rifle. One day, in an ambush, they put a bullet in the priest's eye and he collapsed. The priest's horse wouldn't let the nephew ride him, maybe because he was small and skinny whereas the priest had been big and fat. Then Mr Felipe Neira e Pardo asked to mount the horse, which was a dapple gray, and without dismounting offered the nephew a deal for a gold ounce. When the nephew saw the coin, he took off his beret and said in Basque:

"For the soul of the deceased. Farewell!"

And he headed off to the mountains, with his uncle's gun.

I did, however, meet Don Felipe's son, Teodoro Carlos Neira Xil. He'd already turned sixty. He was bald, of medium height, and had a big nose. He had those blue eyes the native Mirandans have, the ones you so often see in the girls there. He always wore black corduroy, something that really bothers a relative of mine from Vilaverde.

"An heir who looks like a Maragato!" he would say.

Teodoro Carlos had always been a lazy fellow. He kept a knife in his hand and would whittle on a block of wood, carving birds and people with short legs and big heads, all wearing top hats. He'd attended the seminary in Mondoñedo, but our water didn't sit well with him and the Latin didn't let him sleep. In the short time he was there, on the Catherine wheel, he learned several Latin phrases and used them on solemn occasions, like when a legal suit failed or at wakes, creating great silences. One day, on a peak in the mountains, he discovered some strange markings. He carefully cleaned them off with his knife and decided they were letters. He asked me when paper was invented and men stopped writing on rocks.

"There weren't any newspapers then, were there?"

I told him about the small Mesopotamian tablets, papyrus and parchment and the Chinese prisoners from the Battle of Talas, but he either didn't believe all my scientific knowledge or paid no attention, because he had his obsessions. What Teodoro Carlos wanted to know, for example, was how the ancient Galicians sent reports. I asked him to take me to the peak and I'd copy the markings and take the drawing to Charfolé, who was my history professor at the institute in Lugo, and maybe he'd know what they were. He refused, saying it had to do with somebody's honor, or vested interests maybe, and he didn't want it spread around. Then I told him perhaps those writings held the name of some ancient god. This frightened him.

"What if you go there and read it and say the name of the god out loud and he shows up?"

Then he told me about Fuquín the quarryman, who bought some couplets about the madwoman of Barbelle and one night was in his home in Pacios, one night in November – the wind outside was battering the house and it was raining hard and steady – reading the couplets to his family in the kitchen, where they were husking the corn, when he came to the part about Abscóndito the Devil with his big red ears, where bats nested, and his goat legs, which he covered up with some skirts he'd swiped from a lady in Lugo. Fuquín started laughing:

"That Abscóndito!" he said.

At that very moment the window exploded and in came Abscóndito, wrapped all in sparks.

"What's going on here?" bellowed the Devil.

The sparks that accompanied Abscóndito left Fuquín without a stitch of clothing and the pocket watch he had, a Roskoff Patent, melted onto his belly, leaving its mark there, like a tattoo, stopped at seven minutes to eleven.

Neira thought a lot about treasures. He knew how much had to go to the government and consulted a lawyer from Vilalba as to whether the treasures one discovered were taxable or not. One had to pay the government its due. That is to say one thousand five hundred pesetas to kill off the vermin watching over the treasure, a poisonous snake.

"What if a Moor is guarding it?" he asked.

"I wouldn't bill him. He might go to Buenos Aires or Caracas. Then we'd have to put on the receipt: 'Five thousand pesetas to pay the fare of the Moor, who's now in Buenos Aires.'"

As you can see, they were small prices to pay for finding a treasure.

Felipe of Lomba

An American lady in Chicago dreamed about an elephant several nights in a row. The elephant knocked on the door with its trunk, the lady opened and the pachyderm, which was very sophisticated, invited the woman to go for a walk. The woman traveled through the air, riding atop the elephant. One night the woman woke up and there really was somebody knocking on the door of her house. She woke her husband, who got out of bed to see who was banging on the door so loudly and at such an ungodly hour. It was an elephant that had escaped from a circus and was calmly strolling around that neighborhood. The lady recognized it as the elephant of her dreams, the gentle companion that transported her through the air, singing her old English songs just like the ones she would listen to on a record they'd given her for Christmas.

Felipe of Lomba, who was missing an eye because a bur had fallen on him, once went to the wheat harvest in Castile and saw a snakeskin hanging on the door of a church in Santa María de Nieva. It was light green and almost three yards long. Felipe was frightened and for a long time dreamed about the snake from Segovia, how it would coil around his left arm, strike him on the chest and stretch his mouth with its big, frosty tongue. Felipe would wake up and scream and the frightened snake would flee, hitting the floor loudly as it jumped off the bed. There was no doubt about the thud on the floor because by then Felipe was already awake. It was odd that, missing an eye as he was, having lost it as a youth on account of a bur while beating chestnuts off a tree, as I said, he'd seen the snake with both eyes.

Felipe of Lomba consulted a fellow called Chispas of Reiriz, a medicine man with a daughter in Montevideo who could read minds. The daughter had come with an Italian by the name of Paolini to spend a summer in Reiriz and taken advantage of the chance to go to the fairs and earn a lot of money. To start with, Chispas told Felipe to pour flour around his bed so he'd be able to tell where the snake came in and went out. Felipe woke up as usual when the snake was trying to kiss him, heard the thud as the snake fell out of the bed and began to study the trail. It was a hen's tracks, as could clearly be seen by the marks in the flour. Felipe never dreamed about the snake again and dreamed instead about a rooster that pecked and pecked his empty eye socket. He died because he couldn't stand the pain.

"That pecking is driving me crazy!"

"But it isn't real, Felipe! You're dreaming!"

"Well, it still hurts!" he replied.

The rooster's beak pierced and burned him inside like a cattle brand. When Felipe woke up, the rooster would fly away and get into the icebox in the kitchen. Can you believe Felipe found rooster feathers in his icebox more than once?

Chispas of Reiriz ran his right hand over his face, slapped the back of his neck and studied the matter intently.

"He's probably seeing the rooster with the eye he lost, because maybe it's not buried. You can't let an eye walk around in the world by itself!"

Louro of Salceda

Louro lived in Salceda, in that lonely spot on top of the Cordal. His house, always well whitewashed, presided over the walnut trees with its chimney constantly smoking. Louro was thin, of medium height, and had dark hair and restless, black eyes. His hands always moved as he talked, a cigarette butt stuck to his lower lip, moving and spilling ash while he spoke. Louro was always discussing treasures. I had a note with his opinions on it, but lost it and yesterday, while I was shuffling papers around, I found it. Louro knew about a treasure in Fontes, near Parga, which was alone, with no Moor or fairy guarding it. A local from there named Cándido, a bone-setter, discovered it. The treasure spoke to Cándido:

"Hey, Cándido, let me stay in my bed. If you take me out, you'll spend me and if you spend me, how will I look to the other treasures?"

Cándido let himself be persuaded and didn't touch the treasure. Still, he did go to the mountain every year around St Bartholomew and collect the interest. With this money he had a spa treatment in Guitiriz with roast chicken and canned peaches in syrup every day. I asked Louro what Cándido's treasure looked like.

"I can't really tell you, but I think it was a little bit of gold that sat with its back to the door."

Louro was determined to learn to read from right to left so he could talk to the treasures he might find because you have to talk Galician backward to them. For example, "retsim" for "mister," "dlog" for "gold" and "eniw" for "wine."

"And wouldn't a treasure get upset at being called 'retsim'?" I asked him.

"Why?" he replied. "Every language has its own way of saying things!"

Louro told me about a priest who lived in Betanzos and discovered a treasure. The treasure told the priest to turn around because it was going to get its Sunday-go-to-meeting clothes on, since it had been wearing its everyday apparel when it was found. The priest, holding a little mirror in his hand, watched the treasure get dressed. It took off its brown cape, put on a white miter, then grabbed its shadow in both hands and ate it and, along with that, the shadow of a nearby tree. It then stood there shining bright, bright red, in the early evening shadows, among the rocky crags.

"It was a treasure called Paris, the one sometimes mentioned in The Book of St Cyprian," affirmed Louro.

The priest took it home and put it in a glass box. It was a gold mouth with seven teeth. The treasure told the priest it ate words. Every blessed day the priest put a page from Raimundo de Miguel's Latin-Spanish dictionary in its mouth or one from the phone book for Coruña, which he'd stolen from a café in case the treasure wanted to know about people. The priest had to make a trip to Madrid and left the treasure hidden in the stable. When he returned, the treasure had disappeared.

"You can't leave an important person out under the manure, dammit!" was Louro's opinion.

Kathleen March
is Professor of Spanish at the University of Maine, where she specializes in Translation, Galician, Latin American and Women's Studies. She was founder of the International Association of Galician Studies. Her translations into English include the novels *Circling* by Ramón Otero Pedrayo, *Daughter of the Sea* by Rosalía de Castro and *The Inhabited Woman* by Gioconda Belli as well as an anthology of Galician short stories, *Así vai o conto*. She edited an anthology of contemporary Galician women poets, *Festa da palabra*.

GALICIAN

CLASSICS